"You were go... who ran you down in broad daylight? What were you thinking?"

Kim's expression hardened. "I was thinking about the damage that rumors of a hit-and-run by a former resident would do to the manor. I don't expect you to understand, Ethan. You've only been here a day. You couldn't possibly care about the manor's survival the way I do."

The woman was as loyal and compassionate as they came. How could he have suspected her of trying to protect a drug dealer?

"I'm sorry, Kim. I was out of line. Believe me, I want to help you." More importantly, he wanted to get her out of here before the police connected her—or him—to the shooting. The last thing he needed was a cop unraveling his cover. "Come on, I'll drive you home."

In the meantime, he needed descriptions of the kids vandalizing Kim's car, because chances were good one of them had shot Blake, or had seen who did. And Ethan needed to talk to them before the wrong cop got to them. Or Kim.

Witnesses in this case had a bad habit of showing up dead.

Books by Sandra Orchard

Love Inspired Suspense

*Deep Cover
*Shades of Truth

*Undercover Cops

SANDRA ORCHARD

lives in rural Ontario with her real-life hero husband, two of their three children, and a young husky with a fetish for rubber boots and remote controls.

Although Sandra taught high school math before starting her family, her childhood dream of becoming a writer never strayed far from her thoughts. She dabbled in writing how-to articles and book reviews, but for many years, needlecrafts, painting and renovating a century-old farmhouse satisfied her creative appetite.

Then she discovered the world of inspirational fiction, and her writing took on new direction.

In 2009, she won the Daphne du Maurier Award for Excellence in Mystery/Suspense, and the following year, on her "graduation day" as a home-educator (i.e. her youngest daughter's first day of college), Sandra learned that Love Inspired Books wanted to publish her first novel. And so her Undercover Cops series began.

Sandra loves to hear from readers and can be reached through her website, www.SandraOrchard.com, or c/o Love Inspired Books, 233 Broadway, Suite 1001, New York, NY 10279.

SHADES of TRUTH

SANDRA ORCHARD

Love Inspired

™ LOVE INSPIRED BOOKS

Recycling programs
for this product may
not exist in your area.

ISBN-13: 978-0-373-44483-0

SHADES OF TRUTH

Copyright © 2012 by Sandra van den Bogerd

www.LoveInspiredBooks.com

Printed in U.S.A.

The former things will not be remembered,
nor will they come to mind.
—*Isaiah* 65:17

To Kate Weichelt, story doctor extraordinaire
and a real-life heroine, who lost her 20+ year
battle with cancer this past summer.
She remains a true inspiration to all who knew her.

Thanks to

My husband, Michael, for his unwavering support
and encouragement. And to my children.
You're the best!

To Beth Fahnestock, the inspiration
for my heroine's career and the
untiring answerer of all my job-related questions.

To my critiquers and brainstorming buddies,
Kate Weichelt, Vicki Talley McCollum,
Wenda Dottridge and Laurie Benner for their
encouragement and invaluable suggestions.

To my prayer warriors, Angie Breidenbach,
Lisa Jamieson and Patti Jo Moore.

And most importantly, thanks to my Lord Jesus
for the greatest love of all.

ONE

Taking this undercover assignment in Miller's Bay, Ontario, was a bad idea. Too many reminders of his own screwed-up youth.

Ethan Reed trailed Darryl Corbett, the son of the detention facility's founder, into the yard full of teenage boys. The mixed teams of staff and residents on the baseball field underscored the center's buddylike approach to rehabilitation, but the barbed-wire perimeter glinting in the summer sun hammered home the reality.

While Darryl itemized the characteristics that set Hope Manor apart from government-run facilities, Ethan's thoughts drifted to the reason for his secret recruitment from outside the Canadian border town's tight-knit police force. Whoever was luring residents into becoming drug pushers had inside connections. Inside the manor. And inside the police force.

At first glance the youths looked like average kids in their saggy pants and oversize T-shirts, minus iPods dangling from their ears and ball caps askew on their heads. But Ethan didn't miss the hand signals gang members flashed when they thought no one was watching, or the scars on their faces from fighting, or the burns on their skin from initiations.

The facility forbade wearing gang colors, but restrained rivalry was evident in their defiant swaggers and icy stare downs. They tried to look tough, but most of them were cowards who saw nothing wrong with three guys swarming a lone stray, like a pack of wolves circling their dinner.

A foul ball bounced in front of Darryl, who tossed it to the kid on the pitcher's mound. "Basically, you're expected to engage the residents in whatever activities interest them. If you're any good at coaxing them to open up to you and talk out their problems, all the better."

Ethan grunted. He'd better be good at getting the boys to talk, because whoever was recruiting these kids had neglected to mention short life expectancy in the job description.

An engine's roar ricocheted off the brick building. Then a scream—urgent, terrified and female—pierced the air.

Ethan's attention snapped to the perimeter, but a wall of pine trees blocked his view.

"That sounded like Kim," Darryl said. "My sister."

Ethan sprinted for the gate and yanked on the lock. "You got a key?"

"No!" Darryl raced for the building.

Ethan pictured the maze of locked corridors between them and the front exit and dug his fingers into the chain link. "I'll meet you out front." He bolted up the fifteen-foot fence, crushed the slanted barbed wire in his fist and vaulted over the top. Pine needles scratched his arms and face on the way down. He crashed through the trees, cresting the hill in three seconds flat. Not quickly enough to ID the vehicle squealing away. But soon enough to glimpse the blip of its single brake light rounding the corner. A few strides further, he spotted a woman wearing shorts and a sky-blue jogging tank crumpled in the ditch. Her muddied running shoe lay inches from a tire track carved in the dirt.

He skidded down the grassy embankment still slick from last night's storm. A hit-and-run outside his newest undercover gig. Coincidence?

Not if Chief Hanson was right and there was a dirty cop

taking bribes to sabotage the investigation. A cop that had somehow found out about Ethan's mission.

Hitting level ground, Ethan broke into a sprint and grabbed for his phone.

Argh! He didn't have it. A security risk, Darryl had said. A resident might swipe it. Ethan's gaze shot to the driveway. Where was Darryl? They needed to call an ambulance.

Long chestnut hair hid the woman's face, and the image of another jogger slammed into his thoughts. Fifteen years later and he could still picture her broken body. Blocking out the memory, he dropped to his knees at the victim's side.

She appeared to be in her mid-twenties, in remarkable shape, but breathing way too fast and shallow.

"Miss, can you hear me?"

She didn't respond. Didn't move.

And the sight of her motionless body—too much like Joy's—had a stranglehold on his gut. "Miss," he repeated, more urgently this time. "Can you hear me?"

She fixed him with a startled gaze—luminous, rich green and so undeniably alive it kick-started his heart and sent it hurtling into overdrive.

Kim Corbett squeezed her eyes shut and reopened them, but the dark-haired stranger with the shaky voice didn't evaporate. His muscular build blotted out the sun, washing him in a halo of light. Kim blinked again, this time noting the rapid rise and fall of the man's chest, the bunched neck muscles that signaled a readiness to explode into action and, most surprising of all, the look of terror in his dark eyes.

She averted her gaze, swallowed the coppery taste coating her mouth. Ditch water seeped through her shirt and her ankle screamed, but she didn't feel *too* bad. Although, given this guy's worried scrutiny, she must look a mess. She swiped at her mud-streaked hair. "Who are you?"

"Ethan Reed, Hope Manor's new youth-care worker," he

said, and the unexpected hitch in his rumbly voice sent a tingle racing up her spine.

Darryl staggered into her peripheral vision. "You okay?" he asked between gulps of air.

Embarrassed by the fuss she'd caused, she struggled to push onto her elbows.

"Don't move." The man—Ethan—clamped his hands at the base of her skull, rendering her immobile.

"What are you doing?" she shrieked.

"You could have a spinal injury."

"My shift starts in ten minutes. I need to punch in."

"You need to stay still until the paramedics get here."

"Paramedics?" Kim tried to squirm free of Ethan's hold. If he called for paramedics, the police wouldn't be far behind. They'd ask her if she'd recognized the car, the driver. And if they figured out that an ex-resident almost ran her down, it would be the final nail in Hope Manor's coffin.

She couldn't let that happen. Not after Dad had poured his life into this place. "I don't need a paramedic," she protested, but the more she wriggled, the firmer Ethan held her, his hands astonishingly gentle for being so strong.

"Trust me," he said with a gravity that made her stop struggling. "You can never be too careful. What were you doing out here, anyway?"

"I always jog to work when the weather's nice."

The color drained from Darryl's face. "Your neck's bleeding."

"It is?" She reached up to find the source, and Ethan caught her pinky between his first two fingers.

"No," he said, halting her probing with a quick squeeze of his fingers. "It's my hand."

Ignoring the jolt of his touch, she tugged back her hand. "You're bleeding?" she squeaked, and tried again to sit up.

"It's nothing," he said, continuing to brace her neck with that infernally stubborn grip.

"Nothing?" Darryl gaped at Ethan with something akin to awe. "It's a wonder the barbed wire didn't tear your arms to shreds. You're crazy, man. I don't know how you climbed that fence. Everyone's gonna try it now."

Kim gaped. "You climbed the fence?"

Ethan actually blushed, but his eyes never left her face. "Darryl, did you tell someone to call 9-1-1?"

"No, I—"

"The car didn't touch me," Kim said, quickly. "I dove clear when I saw it coming. I'm okay, really."

She'd be even better if they'd just forget the whole thing.

"Humor me until the paramedics get here, okay?"

She took a deep breath, hoping the scent of fresh-mown hay would calm her rattled nerves, but only succeeded in drawing in the musky scent of the man cradling her neck.

His thumb traced the scar along her jaw. And a tiny frown tugged at his lips.

It didn't help that his chocolate-brown eyes radiated protective concern. It was enough to make a girl forget the ache in her ankle, to forget the fear that had flung her into a ditch, even to forget that she was much too busy saving Hope Manor to let her heart flutter over some ruggedly good-looking guy with a surplus of knightlike qualities.

Except, she couldn't forget. The upsurge in drug-related incidents around Miller's Bay had only fueled the lobbying efforts of the people determined to shut down the center.

Instead of running in to call an ambulance, Darryl hunkered down beside her. "Did you see who did this to you?"

"It all happened so fast." She shrank from the memory of the white sports car barreling across the asphalt. No matter how the incident had looked, Blake wouldn't have targeted her deliberately. Never. Why would he want to hurt her?

No reason. None at all.

"You must've seen something," Darryl pressed. "The kind of car? Color?"

Kim glanced nervously at Ethan. "Um, white, I think." She pursed her lips and gave her brother a silent don't-ask-any-more-questions glare, followed by a surreptitious head tilt toward the manor. She grappled to find the newspaper she'd been carrying. One look at the headline and Darryl would guess why she couldn't say anything in front of Ethan.

"I know you're scared," Ethan soothed, apparently misreading her jerky movements, "but every detail you can remember will help the police find this guy. Did you see if the driver was male or female?"

"Male," she said reluctantly. "But I'm sure he didn't see me. He was probably fiddling with his radio. He wouldn't have expected to pass a pedestrian on these back roads."

"You're defending him? He sent you flying into a ditch and didn't even stop to make sure you were okay."

Her cheeks heated at the intensity of Ethan's disapproval. "I'm sure if he'd realized, he would've stopped. No need to make a big deal about this." The slightest negative publicity at this point would destroy any hope of convincing the province to reverse its funding decision.

Ethan's eyes sparked. "What about next time?"

"Next time?"

"Yes. The next time this maniac races down the street, he could send a helpless kid flying into the ditch." Something indefinable flickered across Ethan's face. "And that kid may not be as lucky."

Kim's mouth went dry. Too stunned to respond, she could only stare at him. Was she endangering others by protecting Blake?

Surely not. Whereas the manor's closure might.

Ethan's tone gentled. "What are you afraid of, Kim?"

The low, intimate pitch of his voice trembled through her, warm and soothing, entreating her to trust him. But too much was at stake. She couldn't let him involve the police.

"I'm not afraid. I just overreacted. I told you, I probably

scared the driver more than myself." She twisted sideways, forcing Ethan to loosen his hold. Stones dug into her palms as she scrambled to her feet. Her ankle faltered under her weight, but she stood firm. "I'm fine. See?" She bit the words out through clenched teeth.

"Nevertheless," he said, all traces of warmth gone, "we'll call the police. You may not have seen anything, but I did."

The jump of Kim's pulse at her throat confirmed Ethan's suspicion. She was hiding something. The driver ran her down in broad daylight. An innocent victim would be demanding justice. Never mind that the only information he had for the police was that the culprit's car had a broken taillight. Kim clearly didn't want them to catch the guy.

Something inside Ethan shifted at the obvious implications.

He blew out a breath. When Kim had first opened her eyes, the mix of fear and determination swirling in her gaze had tugged at him in an elemental way he found hard to ignore. But he had a job to do, and the fastest way to deep-six his objectivity was to start caring about the suspects.

Of course, even if Kim weren't a suspect, he'd keep his distance.

She deserved better than the likes of him. His own parents had disowned him after his reckless-driving charge. And his ex-girlfriend had cured him of any illusions that anyone else would ever want him.

Kim shoved her hands into the soggy pockets of her shorts. "I don't see what the police can do. The car didn't hit me."

"So you said." Based on the background checks he'd done, Kim Corbett—daughter of the detention facility's founder, vocal supporter of the facility's mission to rehabilitate young offenders and faithful member of Miller's Bay Community Church—was the last employee of Hope Manor he imagined likely of luring residents into the drug trade.

"What would they arrest him for?" Kim persisted. "Scaring the daylights out of me?"

"How about reckless driving?"

Ethan didn't miss the way Kim's jaw clenched at the suggestion. The only plausible reason she'd cover for the jerk was if she had something bigger to lose.

In the past year, the local cops had identified two former residents of Hope Manor as drug pushers. The pair negotiated a deal to give up the person who'd recruited them in return for a suspended sentence. But neither survived long enough to finger him. Somehow, someone got to them in the jail cell. Which meant whoever was behind the operation would stop at nothing to ensure his anonymity.

And maybe Kim knew it. Maybe this was a warning to keep her mouth shut, or else.

Ethan winced at the thought. Okay, so forget calling the police. He'd handle this himself.

Darryl nudged his sister to start walking. "Let's get you ice for that ankle and into dry clothes before we worry about anything else."

Despite her earlier bravado, Kim gingerly avoided putting her full weight on her left foot.

Thankful that at least she didn't have a spinal injury, Ethan dragged in his first full breath since finding her sprawled in the ditch. He may have relinquished his hold on her, but the tension in his muscles took longer to let go. This guy had some sort of control over her, and if Ethan wanted to win her confidence enough to learn what it was, he might as well forget about keeping his distance.

The rustle of a dirt-smeared newspaper caught his attention. "Is this yours?" he called after Kim, and then stooped to retrieve the paper. The headline—Funding Cuts Threaten Detention Center's Future—dominated the page.

The instant Darryl scanned the headline, his eyes darkened. "Please tell me you aren't hatching another one of your schemes." At Ethan's raised eyebrow, Darryl explained. "Our dad founded this place, and as the oldest child, Kim seems to think she has a sacred duty to save it."

Kim gasped. "How can you say that?"

Another reason crossed Ethan's mind. Closing the manor would dry up a ready supply of eager recruits.

Kim met his gaze. "Is it so wrong to not want to see my father's work lost?"

"No, I think it's admirable."

Kim shot her brother a smug grin.

Ethan chuckled at Darryl's snort. Joining Kim's cause might be the perfect opportunity to get closer to her and, more importantly, closer to the truth. He tucked the newspaper under his arm and fell into step beside her. "How do you plan to save Hope Manor from the chopping block?"

"I want to get a petition together to pressure the provincial government to reconsider," Kim explained. "And I want to pitch an idea to the newspaper for a series on former residents who've made good. Once people see the impact we have, I'm sure they'll support our petition."

"You'll only make the situation worse." Darryl swiped his pass card over the lock to the staff entrance and opened the door. Chilled air spilled out, but the crisp blast did nothing to cool the heat in his voice. "Half the people in this town didn't know there was a detention center here until you wrote that letter to the editor a few weeks back."

Kim eased onto one of the benches lining the space between the walls of lockers and unlaced her shoe. "That's why they need to hear its success stories."

"Trust me. They don't want to know that Miller's Bay harbors young offenders. Involve the papers and it's only a matter of time before the incident with Mitch gets out, too."

"The Mitch I was hired to replace?" Ethan asked, surprised they'd managed to suppress the news this long in such a small town. The town's size had been one of the reasons he'd been recruited for this assignment from outside the local force.

"Yeah," Darryl said. "He got injured chasing a resident who ran off during a field trip."

"Ouch, not the kind of news that will endear Hope Manor to the citizens of Miller's Bay."

Darryl shot his sister a look. "Exactly."

"I won't give up, Darryl. Dad poured his life into this place, because he believes in God's forgiveness. These kids need to know that even if they repeatedly mess up, God will forgive them, too."

Kim reminded him of Joy. Despite the pain he'd caused her, she'd offered him that kind of forgiveness. And because of her, he devoted his life to ridding the streets of people like the irresponsible teenager he'd been. While Kim worked to set them free.

What he needed to know was…did she work out of compassion, or to sideline in something more lucrative?

Because, if she was on the level, why had someone just tried to kill her?

TWO

"Change out of those wet clothes while I grab you an ice pack and find Ethan a bandage for his hand," Kim's brother said, unlocking the hall door.

Ethan gave the room one last surreptitious scan before stepping into the empty corridor. Aside from the feeling in his gut, he had little evidence the attack on Kim was deliberate, let alone connected to his case. But at least no one could get to her in the locked room.

The main floor of the facility was divided into three units that each housed ten residents and a staff station. Ethan turned left toward the closest. "I'd sure like to get my hands on whoever ran down your sister," he said, hoping to loosen Darryl's tongue.

Darryl caught him by the shoulder and swung him around. "Don't even think about messing with my sister."

Ethan whacked off the guy's hold. "What are you talking about?"

"I saw the way you looked at her. You're here to do a job. Not cozy up to Kim."

Ethan backed up a step and lifted his hands in innocence. "Hey, I just want to catch the jerk who scared her."

A door clicked and Darryl's gaze snapped to the end of the hall.

The manor's interim director, Aaron Sheppard, hurried

toward them. Ethan fought not to gag at the overpowering scent of the thirty-year-old's trendy cologne. Or maybe it was the smell of the gunk he used to make his hair poke out in that wannabe-actor look. His too blue eyes—had to be colored contacts—zeroed in on Darryl. "How's Kim? I heard she had an accident."

Darryl stopped the guy from pushing his way into the locker room. "She was jogging and twisted her ankle. She'll be fine. Her ankle just needs a little icing."

"But someone said—"

"She's embarrassed enough," Darryl interrupted, apparently more concerned about guarding his sister than ticking off his boss. "She doesn't need people yakking about her."

Aaron drew in a breath as if he intended to argue, but then his gaze shifted to Ethan. He thrust out his hand. "Ethan, right? Welcome aboard."

Ethan matched his firm grip, noting the way Aaron's gaze returned to the staff room door, and then to Darryl. Definitely another man worth grilling for information.

"Was there something else?" Darryl said.

"Yeah, you've got a phone message. Wanted you to call back ASAP."

Worry replaced Darryl's scowl. "The hospital?"

"Not sure. While you're in the office, let the in-charge supervisor know that she needs to call someone to cover Kim's shift."

"Kim won't like being sent home, but it's probably not a bad idea. Could you show Ethan where he can get the ice?" Darryl's gaze shifted to Ethan. "Then I'll meet you back here to finish the orientation."

After Darryl disappeared down the corridor, Ethan took advantage of the opportunity to ply Aaron for information. "Who's in the hospital?"

"His dad. Cancer. Admitted on the weekend. The pain got to be too much. It's only a matter of time now." Aaron paused outside the door of unit one's staff station. "I heard what you said about catching the guy who ran Kim down. So she didn't *just* twist her ankle jogging?"

"No, sir."

"Did you see the guy?"

"Unfortunately not. You got any idea who it might've been?"

"Some kid out bah-hawing, I expect." Aaron's lips pressed into a flat line as if he might have a particular kid in mind. He unlocked the door to the staff station—a glass-walled peninsula from which the entire unit could be viewed. Each unit consisted of a common room with a nailed-down sofa, TV and game tables, a washroom, a laundry room and a line of bedrooms, lockable only from the outside. The residents were in morning classes, so the unit was empty.

"You get a lot of kids from the area driving crazy on these back roads?"

"You know how it is. Boys will be boys."

"Hmm." Ethan found the first-aid kit and swabbed his palm with disinfectant.

Aaron pulled a bag of ice from a small fridge in the corner, and then waved to a plate of muffins on the desk. "Help yourself. Kim's mom is always baking for the staff and residents. How she copes with stress, Mr. Corbett once told me." Aaron rubbed his stomach. "I think we've all gained ten pounds since he took ill." He handed Ethan the ice. "Here you go. Can you find your own way back?"

"Sure, but—" Ethan's gaze flicked to the glass partition. His mind buzzed with possible reasons Aaron might want to hang back in an empty unit. None of them aboveboard. "Didn't you want to see Kim?"

Aaron unlocked the door and motioned him to exit. "I'll see her later, tonight."

Ethan frowned. Not that who Kim saw in her free time was any of his business…unless the person was connected to his case, which Aaron very well could be. It was more believable than thinking Kim was on the wrong side of the law.

But before Ethan could ask another question, Aaron prodded him out the door. *Definitely suspicious.* Ethan hurried to the locker room. At least with Darryl fielding a phone call, he'd get his chance to question Kim alone.

Raised voices stopped his hand midknock. Two voices. One female—Kim's. One male.

He strained to hear what they were saying, but the male voice dropped to an angry hiss.

"No—" Kim cried, and slamming of metal on metal swallowed the rest of her words.

Ethan twisted the knob uselessly and pounded the door. "Hey, open up."

The door jerked open, and Kim's brother stood on the other side, teeth gritted.

Because of the phone call? Or something else?

Ethan pushed his way inside, his gaze sweeping the room. "What's going on?"

"I'm being sent home." Kim hooked a padlock onto the door he'd heard slam, and then stalked to a wooden bench. She'd changed into a fresh green T-shirt that did amazing things for her eyes. Or maybe the disagreement with her brother had brought out those fiery flecks.

Darryl snatched up the ice bag and tossed it to Kim. "Now keep that foot elevated until Ginny gets here." He ignored Kim's long-suffering sigh. "Come on, Ethan. I'll take you to admissions. We have a resident due back from court. I can show you how we process arrivals."

Terrific. He'd have to bide his time until he got another chance to interrogate Kim.

A crackly voice shouted, "Yard. Now," over Darryl's walkie-talkie.

Kim scooped the ice bag off her foot. "Go ahead, Darryl. Ethan and I can handle the incoming."

Ethan reached to help her up, but she brushed his hand aside, as if her injury was of no concern.

"When an incident with a resident escalates," she explained, leading the way through the maze of corridors, "you shout *now* and your location into your walkie-talkie to summon help. It doesn't happen that often, but between my taking up yours and Darryl's time and Tony off, we're a little short staffed."

"Who's Tony?"

"One of our full-timers. He called in sick just before his shift this morning."

This morning, huh? Ethan made a mental note to look up Tony's address and pay him a visit. Check out his taillights. "Has he worked here long?"

"Since the place opened."

"That long? He must've been upset when the board hired a new guy as deputy director instead of promoting senior staff." Maybe upset enough to look at making some money on the side with a homegrown drug ring.

She shrugged, but her puckered brow suggested the possibility bothered her. Or was it the manor's uncertain future?

"Here we are." She unlocked the admission room connected to a sally port—an entrance rigged to secure the outer door before the inner door opened.

The musty odor that seeped into the corridor resurrected memories he'd willed himself to forget. He braced his hands on the door frame, one foot bridging the threshold, the other cemented to the hall. He felt sixteen again, teetering on the edge of a sinkhole that threatened to swallow him from the inside out. The humiliation of being restrained. The loneliness as weeks passed without a visitor. The remorse that gnawed at him day and night.

"Ethan? Are you okay?"

Kim's voice jerked him back to the present. "Yes." He gave his head a hard shake. "Yes, I'm fine."

"Is it your hand?"

"What?" He pulled his hand from the door frame and looked at the bandage. Come to think of it, it was throbbing.

"Maybe you should have the nurse—"

"It's fine." He stepped into the room and moved toward the window overlooking the attached garage. If he expected to gain her trust, he needed to utilize every available minute, not fuss over a couple of puncture wounds.

"Sounds like my bigger concern should be how long my new job's gonna be around." He propped his hip on the side of the desk. "Maybe I should help you with your petition."

"Really?"

"Sure." The sun seemed to rise in her eyes, and Ethan regretted that his offer had more strings attached than a trussed-up turkey. "Although I am curious why your brother is opposed to the idea. Is that what had him so riled back there?"

Kim sank wearily into the chair. "I don't know. He used to talk to me, but lately…" Her gaze shifted to the thick-paned window. "I guess we all deal with grief in our own way."

"I heard your father has cancer, and that it's bad. I'm sorry." Hoping he wasn't pushing his luck, Ethan reached out and squeezed her shoulder. "Darryl will come around. You'll see." The slight relaxing of her muscles beneath his fingers left him fighting the temptation to let his hand linger. He took a step back. "So, who do we have coming in?"

"Um, I think it's Mel." She double-checked the sign-in book. "Yes, Melvin Reimer."

"What can you tell me about him?"

"He's fifteen. A good kid, really. Comes from a stable family, but he had a hard time making friends at school."

"Let me guess. He got sucked into a gang."

"Yeah, but I've been urging him to get out."

"The gang's not going to let that happen."

"It's not their choice. It's his. And he's matured a lot in the months he's been here, which is only one example of why it's so important to do everything we can to make sure the government doesn't shut us down."

Ethan chose not to dispute the Pollyanna view. Her optimism was kind of refreshing. "Did Melvin have a parole hearing this morning?"

"No, a group conference between his family and the victim's. This was a big step for him. He wanted the opportunity to apologize, ask for forgiveness and achieve some sort of reconciliation."

"Wow, that takes guts."

The rumble of the garage door rattled the windows. A police cruiser pulled inside. After the door closed behind the vehicle, the officer extracted a tall, lanky kid from the backseat, his hands and feet shackled.

Kim pushed to her feet, a proud smile curving her lips. "The kids call him Beanpole."

"What's he in for?"

She jabbed the button that opened the admission room door. "He got drunk, stole a car and smashed through a neighbor's living-room window. Wounded their four-year-old daughter."

Ethan swallowed the sour taste that rose to his throat as the kid shuffled across the cement, his head down. "Today's meeting must've been tough for...everyone."

"Yeah, but you know what they say. What doesn't kill you makes you stronger."

"Like the car that almost took you out this morning?"

She waved off the question and turned to the kid coming through the door.

Ethan kneaded the tension at the back of his neck. His protective instincts had kicked into high gear the moment he'd heard her scream, and they hadn't let up in the hour since. He couldn't remember the last time he'd met a more stubborn woman. Some guy had tried to run her off the road, and she acted as though it was no big deal.

The question was, *why?* Because Ethan's gut told him she couldn't be more wrong.

At the sight of her friend Ginny pulling up to the curb, Kim walked out the staff exit, hyperaware of Ethan's nearness. He was being so sweet—offering to help with her petition, sympathizing with Dad's condition, seeing her to the car—that she didn't know how to act. Was he interested in her?

Or was he just a supernice guy?

At least she managed not to limp. She'd probably break out in a silly grin if he actually offered her an arm to lean on. And the curious glint in Ginny's eye didn't help.

With how kind Ethan had been, Kim felt guilty for not admitting that she knew who almost ran her down. But Blake had spent sixteen months at Hope Manor. If the police hauled him in for dangerous driving, not only would the news fuel the arguments for shutting down the manor, the arrest would set him back years. And after the protective way Ethan had pounded on the locker room door when Darryl was yelling at her, she was pretty sure that if she told him about Blake, he would send the police to the guy's doorstep before his name left her mouth.

It was bad enough she'd let Darryl needle the admission out of her. At least he'd agreed not to involve the police. Of course, his insistence that she take the day off still irked. The swelling in her ankle had almost disappeared. But at least this way she'd have the chance to deal with Blake sooner rather than later. "Thanks so much for coming to get me, Ginny," she said as they neared the car.

"No problem." Ginny's speculative gaze shifted to Ethan. "You must be the new guy who came to Kim's rescue."

"The name's Ethan." He extended his hand, and Ginny gave it a hearty workout.

Kim hid a smile. Her friend held to the theory that you could tell a lot about a person from their handshake. A limp one was a particularly bad sign, but from the approving grin Ginny shot her, Ethan must've passed muster.

"Have you been in town long, Ethan?" Ginny asked.

"Since last weekend. I moved down from Toronto." Ethan opened the passenger door.

As Kim stepped past him, trying to ignore the rock-solid build that had vaulted a fifteen-foot fence to dash to her rescue, she felt that familiar rush of new-crush excitement.

"Did you work at a detention center in Toronto before this?" Ginny asked.

"Nope. I was a police officer."

Kim's heart hiccupped. "A police officer? And you quit? What happened?"

His shrug was nonchalant, but the flush inching up his neck suggested he felt anything but. "I was looking for a change. Tired of the big city."

"Ignore her," Ginny said, climbing into the driver's seat. "She has this thing for guys in uniform."

"Me? You're the one who married a cop."

Ethan flashed them an amused grin that crinkled the corners of his eyes. "I think that's my cue to get back to work. Now, make sure you stay off that foot," he reminded before closing the car door. Despite the ninety-degree heat, he waited at the curb until they drove away.

"He seems nice," Ginny said.

Kim smothered a bubbly squeal. "You should've seen the way he took charge when he found me in the ditch. He was so afraid I'd broken my neck that he wouldn't let me move."

"A man who can keep you down? Wow, that's a first."

"Ha, ha. Very funny." Kim propped her foot on the dash and examined her ankle.

Ginny glanced from the road to Kim. "You *like* him."

Kim tried not to squirm. "Sure, he's nice," she said, and not wanting to admit to anything more, quickly added, "I wonder why he quit police work."

"He told you."

"Not really. He could've gotten a job on a small-town police force if he just wanted out of the big city. I think something bad must've happened to him."

"Of course you do," Ginny said in her indulgent, eye-roll voice.

"I'm serious. Maybe he got shot. Or maybe he shot someone and couldn't cope with the emotional fallout."

"Or…" Ginny said, stretching out the word for effect. "Maybe he wants a quieter life away from the big city and *nosy* females."

Kim poked out her tongue. "Your marrying a cop has taken all the fun out of our guy talks. You do know that?"

"You're interested in this guy?" Ginny's gaze flicked from the road to Kim. "I thought you were dating Aaron. Which is a wonder in itself considering that since Nate, you haven't dated anyone for longer than two weeks."

Heat blazed through Kim's chest and flamed into her face, the flare instant and embarrassing. She dropped her foot to the floor with a thunk, cranked up the air-conditioning. "Nate who? I never *dated* anyone named Nate. Oh…" She covered a mocking gasp. "You mean that guy who *courted* me for eight months and then married my college roommate?"

Ginny's voice softened. "Kim, don't. You don't have to pretend with me."

"Who's pretending? I dated Zach for four weeks. That's a lot longer than two. And Aaron is just a friend."

His touch sure didn't zing up her arms the way Ethan's had.

"And if this Ethan asks you out, you'll keep him around for what, six weeks? And then what, Kim?" Ginny's eyes hardened with determination. "You can't keep punishing yourself, and other men, because of Nate."

"I'm not." Kim shifted her attention to a passing truck. "I just don't have time to date."

Ginny's voice sobered. "I guess you saw today's paper."

"Yeah, but I hope Dad didn't." The possibility tied her in knots. "If the cancer weren't already killing him, today's headline would."

Ginny turned onto Kim's street. The yards, normally filled with laughing children, lay as desolate in the sweltering heat as her family home had felt since she'd moved back to help care for Dad.

"I hate to bring this up on top of everything else going on right now," Ginny said. "But the youth pastor was hoping you could give another talk about the dangers of drug use, maybe talk about what it's like for the kids at Hope Manor. Give them a picture of where a little 'innocent' fun can lead. He's worried about one girl in particular, but doesn't want to single her out in case he's wrong." Ginny parked in the driveway. "And from what Rick tells me about the recent rise in drug-related crimes, all the kids need to be warned."

"Your hubby's right. They do. I'd be happy to speak to the group."

A new fear pinched Kim's throat. What if Blake was high when he gunned his car at her?

If he was using again, he might not respond well to being confronted. But she couldn't pretend the incident never happened. If he'd merely been distracted, she'd warn him to be more careful. If he was using...

Her finger strayed to the scar under her jaw, courtesy of the last drug user she'd tried to reason with. She'd met the kid while he was doing a stint at the manor. He'd been a good kid, considering. When she'd happened upon him a year later smoking crack in an empty picnic pavilion at Harbor Park, the red gang bandanna around his arm should've clued her in to how much he'd changed. She hadn't noticed his knife until he rounded the table, enraged by her audacity to tell him he was screwing up his life. He'd grabbed her hair and scraped the blade across her throat.

An icy chill shivered down her spine.

Stop it. Nothing was going to happen. She yanked an elastic from the pocket of her shorts and wound her hair into a tight bun, just in case. Maybe she should ask someone to go with her.

She glanced at Ginny.

No, she could no more confide in her wife-of-a-cop friend than in her overprotective Good Samaritan. Ginny would try to talk her out of it, and then she'd sic her hubby on Blake. And as much as Kim trusted Rick's discretion, she couldn't risk talk that would further blacken the manor's reputation. She swallowed, and dread sank like a stone to the pit of her stomach.

She had no choice. She'd face Blake alone.

THREE

Never more relieved to see a shift end, Ethan grabbed his cell phone and wallet from his locker and headed for the car. The muggy air sat heavy in his chest, kind of like his day.

Being here had scraped open so many memories he felt raw.

He'd done his job—acquainted himself with the facility and their procedures, introduced himself to the daytime staff and met the residents. But he'd struggled to stay focused. The incident involving Kim presented the most promising lead, and all he'd wanted to do was follow up on it.

Reaching his car, he pulled out his phone to check the internet for her address. As the info came up, Aaron Sheppard exited the building, phone pressed to his ear.

Head down, Aaron strode toward the parking lot, talking intently.

Ethan hoped Aaron wasn't solidifying plans to get together with Kim, because Ethan planned to stop by her place on the pretense of checking on her ankle. And he didn't want the other man in the way, especially since he didn't intend to leave until he figured out what she was hiding.

He opened his car door to a blast of heat that tripled the sweat sluicing down his neck. The A/C in the cheap apartment he'd rented on the east side of town had better work better tonight than it had last night or he could forget about getting any sleep. Once he wrapped up this case, he'd work on finding a house with central air, a decent yard. Maybe adopt a dog.

Two cars over, Aaron revved the engine of his green Mini Cooper and slammed down his phone. A moment later, he roared out of the parking lot, tires squealing.

Curious about what got him so riled, Ethan shoved his stick shift into First and followed.

Aaron hit Lakeshore Road and turned east toward Harbor Park. Ethan hung back so as not to be spotted.

The car circled the packed parking lot and squeezed into a space only a Mini Cooper would fit into. Ethan pulled up onto the grass three rows over.

The air smelled of heated sand and coconut oil. Sunbathers crammed the beach. Squealing children romped in the cool Lake Erie water.

Aaron shaded his eyes and scanned the crowds. He headed for a spreading maple where a group of young people huddled around a picnic table.

Ethan shed his shirt to blend in with the beachgoers and moseyed to a nearby bench.

A blonde, no more than fifteen, pushed a paper bag across the table to Aaron.

The scene had *drug deal* written all over it. Except the girl didn't have the cocky attitude of an experienced seller. Her hands trembled and her gaze never lifted past the middle of Aaron's chest.

Aaron peeked inside the bag, his expression neutral. Then he scrunched the top of the bag in his fist and said something Ethan couldn't make out.

Ethan pulled out his cell phone and, pretending to search for a signal, snapped pictures of the three girls and two guys hanging on to Aaron's every word. Everyone appeared more relaxed now that the exchange had been made.

People usually didn't hang around to talk after a drug buy. So what was in the bag?

The teens moved toward the pier, and Aaron headed back to the parking lot. But he walked past his car.

Ethan maneuvered through the playground, keeping Aaron in his sights.

Aaron crossed the sidewalk in front of the ice-cream shop, but instead of going inside, he skulked along the side of the building and slipped in behind.

Ethan snuck behind the neighboring building and scaled a stack of skids in time to glimpse Aaron toss the bag in a Dumpster.

A dead drop?

Ethan ducked before Aaron could spot him. He peered through the slatted fence separating the buildings.

Seagulls screeched overhead.

Ethan shrank into the shadows, but Aaron didn't pay the noisy birds any attention. He brushed off his hands and sauntered back toward the parking lot.

As much as Ethan wanted to follow, he needed to see what was in that bag. He edged along the fence and scanned the area for signs of anyone who might be there to make the pickup. Whoever it was wouldn't wait too long or he'd risk the bag getting buried.

The rear door of the ice cream shop opened and a teenage boy in a white apron and hairnet hauled out a trash bag. He set the bag on the cement stoop and pulled out a smoke.

Was this the pickup guy?

The kid lit up and started texting on his cell phone. Sweat glistened on his face, but that was as likely from the heat as nerves.

Ethan swiped his shirt over his own damp face, and then pulled the shirt back on.

The kid snapped shut his phone and ground his cigarette butt under his heel. As he reached for the door handle, he seemed to remember the trash bag. He opened the Dumpster and tossed in the bag without so much as glancing under the lid.

Ethan shifted his position for a better view and spotted Aaron's Mini speeding off. If only he could be in two places at once...

Ethan forced himself to wait. Sweat trickled down his spine. Every muscle tensed, ready to spring into action.

Five minutes passed. But no one else appeared.

Ethan squeezed past a loose board on the fence and ran for the cover of the Dumpster. He waited another full minute, scanning for any sign he'd been spotted. Seeing none, he lifted the lid.

The putrid odor of marinating garbage knocked him back.

Holding his breath, he ignored the burn of the black metal against his palms, and crawled over the side of the bin.

Aaron's bag sat perched on a bed of trash.

Ethan snatched it up, slammed down the lid and sucked in a breath. Crouching beside the bin, he checked again to ensure no one was looking, then opened the bag.

It held two packets of white powder.

Ethan stared at the packets in confusion. If the rendezvous back there was what it looked like, why'd Aaron toss the drugs?

Had the handoff been some kind of test?

Ethan mentally reviewed what he knew about the man. A degree in community justice. Nine years' experience at the Hamilton youth detention center with an exemplary record. Although twice he'd applied to the police force and had been passed over.

On Mr. Corbett's recommendation, Hope Manor's board had hired Aaron as deputy director eight months ago. Now Mr. Corbett's sudden turn for the worse had spring-boarded Aaron to the manor's top position, surpassing not only senior employees, but the founder's two children.

Not that Kim appeared to hold any resentment.

On the contrary, if Aaron's "I'll see her tonight" could be believed, Kim considered him a friend. Maybe more than a friend.

Ethan crushed the bag in his fist and hurried to his car. He needed to know what Kim knew about Aaron Sheppard.

The instant the front door closed, Kim bolted from the couch. She'd thought Ginny would never go home.

Kim grabbed her car keys and headed for the door. If she didn't hurry, Darryl would catch her leaving. He'd be so livid, she'd never make it to Blake's.

Working with the residents to help them reach for a better life was so much a part of who they were, she couldn't understand why Darryl wasn't as determined as her to safeguard Dad's legacy.

Kim drove to the east side of town where Blake shared a row house with his older brother. The nearby candy factory was the sole remnant of the neighborhood's economic glory days. And as she pulled onto their street, the sickeningly sweet scent of gumdrops hung so thick in the air she could taste it.

Dingy stucco houses squatted feet from the sidewalk, their porch roofs drooping over sagging front porches as if sinking into a drunken stupor.

The odd boarded-up window added to the effect. While duct tape crisscrossed others like slashes on a desperate teen's wrists.

Driveways were conspicuously absent. Instead, scraggly hedges offered what meager privacy was to be had from encroaching neighbors.

Here and there a rusted-out pickup languished at the curb. The sole sign of prosperity until a gust of wind chased a crumpled fast-food bag up the street and into…Blake's white sports car.

Kim's heart jerked. No one in this end of town drove a car like that unless they were dealing drugs.

She tightened her grip on the steering wheel and pulled to a stop. How had she thought she could do this?

She dropped her forehead to her hands and gave in to the shakes that had dogged her all day. Maybe Ethan was right. Maybe she should've called the police.

His troubled voice whispered through her mind. *What are you afraid of, Kim?*

She sucked in a breath. She wasn't afraid. Not of anything Blake might do to her. Not really. She was well trained in self-defense. Not that she'd need to use it. She was here to talk.

Nothing more.

So why was she still trembling?

She pictured Dad lying in his hospital bed. She couldn't fail him. She wouldn't. Clasping her hands, she prayed the words she'd heard her father pray time and again. *Lord, please let Blake see Your love in me.*

Strengthened by the prayer, Kim stepped out of the car and limped toward Blake's house.

The ping of a stone drew her around. But no one was there. Not on the sidewalk. Not in the minuscule weed-infested yards. Not in…

She tried to peer through the windshields of the pick-ups parked along the street, and through the windows of the houses, but the reflections made seeing anything impossible.

Despite temperatures that could fry an egg, a shiver fingered the back of her neck. She told herself she was being paranoid.

Even so, she clawed her keys between the fingers of her right hand and palmed her cell phone in her left.

Shouting cut into her thoughts.

Her pulse quickened. The voice sounded like Darryl's.

She traced the sound to an open window at the side of Blake's house, well back from the street. She should've known Darryl intended to confront Blake himself when he agreed so easily not to involve the police.

She edged closer, staying out of sight of the window.

Blake said something she couldn't make out, and Darryl exploded into a rage. "If I see you within a mile of my sister, you'll be looking at the inside of a jail cell so fast your head'll spin."

Blake laughed. A scoffing, ugly sound. "I go down, you go down. You hear what I'm saying?"

Shock trapped Kim's breath in her throat. What did Blake mean?

He couldn't possibly have anything on her brother. Darryl might have his faults—like being overprotective—but he was as honest as they came.

Darryl never should've told Blake they were related. They always operated on a first-name basis with residents, precisely to avoid these kinds of threats. How many times had Dad drilled that into them?

She slumped against the wall, sending an empty beer can toppling from the window ledge to the cement slab below. She froze.

"What was that noise?" Blake demanded. Chair legs abruptly scraped the floor.

Kim sprang to her feet and sprinted toward the street. Her ankle screamed, but instinct propelled her. Never mind that Darryl would never let Blake hurt her.

The keys dug into her clenched fist. Her heart pounded in her ears. She heard a sound behind her. But she didn't dare glance back.

She cleared the hedge bordering the yard and skidded to a stop.

Two grungy-looking punks were circling her car. Slowly. Deliberately. Peering in windows. Trying the doors. One of them—a pockmarked teen with jeans sagging to his knees— slapped a baseball bat against his palm, looking ready to take a swing at her windshield.

Icy fear shot through her veins. She backed up a step.

Shades of Truth

The second kid crouched next to her tires and pulled a knife from his pocket.

Behind her a door slammed. Darryl?

She opened her mouth to yell for help, but the word died in her throat. So far those punks hadn't seen her. Better to keep it that way.

A truck roared to life.

"There she is," the kid with the knife yelled.

Baseball Bat shot her a poisonous glare.

For an instant she froze, stunned by the seething hatred in his eyes. How did they know her? What did they want?

Too late she turned and cried out. Her brother was speeding away.

The punks chewed the distance between them.

She ducked behind the hedge and scrabbled down Blake's side yard. Her ankle throbbed. Shallow breaths from her throat. She should have listened to Ethan.

Footfalls pounded behind her. Louder. Closer. Matching the frantic beat of her heart.

The instant she passed the house, Blake's rear screen door slapped open. "Hey, what's going on?"

Kim cut across a neighboring yard to the next street. Sweat dripped into her eyes, burning them. She couldn't run much longer. Her gaze darted from side to side, desperately seeking a hiding place. The candy factory's near-empty parking lot swam in her vision. "Help!" she screamed.

Fifty yards ahead of her a dark figure exploded from the bushes.

No. No. *No!* She veered left and raced across the deserted street. Her ankle turned on a pothole. Searing pain cut off her breath, hauling her to a stop.

A gunshot cracked the air.

Expecting to feel the sting of a bullet, she dove for the dirt. Her phone flew out of her grip, skidded across the scalding blacktop.

A merciless hand closed around her arm and yanked her to her feet.

Desperate to break free, she flailed her arms and drew breath to scream.

Her assailant slapped his palm over her mouth, pulled her head against his rock-hard chest. "Quiet," he growled. He clamped his other arm around her middle, pinning her arms to her side, and dragged her into the overgrown bushes bordering the candy factory.

She fought for air, struggling all the harder against his iron grip.

Branches clawed at her hair. Thorny twigs scratched her face.

Suddenly, she remembered the keys spiked through her fingers, and speared them into his thigh.

He roared, but his grip didn't slacken.

FOUR

Ethan bit back a curse as Kim's foot glanced off his shin. He tightened his hold on her and peered through the trees. The gunshots had stopped. No sign of anyone looking for them. The chaotic pounding in his chest slowed a fraction.

"Kim, it's Ethan. I won't hurt you." He turned her sideways, keeping his hold firm so she couldn't bolt into the shooter's sights.

The instant she saw his face the panic in her eyes flashed to relief, then white-hot anger. She lashed her arms free of his grip. "What are you doing here?"

He lifted his hands, palms out, to assure he meant no harm. "I live down the street, heard you scream." Her cry had ripped through his chest like buckshot. He expected her to be falling apart, not taking a strip out of him. "When I saw you go down, my only thought was to get you to cover."

Her gaze rested a moment on his bandaged left hand. Her rapid breathing began to slow. "You live in this neighborhood?" she said, her voice a mixture of surprise and repugnance.

Her tone, so similar to his ex-girlfriend's after he'd told her about his stint in detention, made the back of his neck prickle. "What are *you* doing here?" he demanded, his anger at her for putting herself in danger making the question sound harsher than he'd intended.

He'd driven by her house and found it empty. A neighbor said she was probably at the hospital with her dad. But deep down, he'd feared that whoever came after her this morning would try again.

"I caught a couple of kids vandalizing my car. What kind of stupid thrill is it to slash someone's tires and smash their windshield? They won't think it's so fun when they wind up in jail. Let me tell you."

He scraped a hand through his hair. Two attacks in one day couldn't be a coincidence. Someone wanted her out. And he didn't have a clue who. "What were you doing here in the first place?"

She averted her gaze the same way she had when she'd hedged his questions this morning.

How was he supposed to protect her if she didn't tell him what was really going on?

"I came to visit a...friend."

"Then why didn't you run to her house?"

"They came at me so fast. I didn't have time to think. I just ran."

"Usually when kids are caught vandalizing property they scram. You didn't recognize them?"

"No, but they seemed—" she hesitated, and at the raw fear in her eyes, his irritation over her secretiveness evaporated "—to know me. Or at least, that I owned the car."

"They probably watched you park." Not that it explained why they'd chase her, let alone shoot at her. What kind of "friend" was she here to visit?

Her face was white, her lips pinched tight, and from the way she shifted all her weight to her uninjured ankle she looked as though she was in serious pain.

He pointed to a rusty, overturned barrel behind her. "Sit for a minute."

In the distance, sirens blared.

"Someone must've called in the gunshot." He cocked his

head. "Sounds like police and ambulance. Did you see who had the gun?"

"No. I didn't see any gun. They were carrying a bat and knife."

He looked around at the tattered houses with their boarded-up windows and curling shingles. Crushed beer cans littered dirt-patched yards. "Maybe the shot had nothing to do with you, then." He hoped. Graffiti—sick slurs and even sicker images—defaced the factory wall. "This neighborhood attracts more than its share of crime."

"You mean someone out there is taking potshots at people?"

He shrugged. "It happens." He offered her a hand. "Come on."

She hesitated a moment, and when she finally slipped her hand in his it felt oddly dainty. Dainty, yes, but when she leaned into his support and rose he could also feel the thread of steely determination that ran through her. The connection of their joined hands gave him a feeling of…rightness.

He ignored the irrational thought as she tested her injured ankle, resisting the urge to wrap his arm around her waist and carry her. "We'll check over your car and give the police a description of the vandals," he said brusquely. "Then you need to go home and rest."

From the cover of the trees, Ethan scanned the vicinity for signs of the punks and squinted at every window for evidence of a sniper. Red-and-blue emergency lights from the next street strobed across the dead space between the houses. "If those punks have a brain in their heads, they'll be long gone by now," he said, sweeping the branches out of Kim's way. "Can you manage with that foot?"

"Yeah, I'll be okay." She took a step, barely concealing a wince. She tugged her bottom lip between her teeth.

"You stay put and I'll bring your car here. Where are you parked?"

"On the next street, but—" Her gaze darted from the factory

to the row of run-down houses and back to him. She looked scared.

"Or we can cut through those yards."

"That would be better."

Supporting her weight as much as she'd allow, he forced himself to focus on helping her to her car, instead of the feel of her body leaning against his.

They crossed the street and shuffled down the alley between two houses. As they reached the backyards, Kim's hand suddenly clenched. Her face went white.

Paramedics were loading a man onto a gurney. White gauze, stained red at the man's temple, circled his head. A spent casing, flagged by police, lay in the dirt ten feet away.

"Looks like we've found the gunshot victim," Ethan said. "At least this means the shot wasn't intended for you."

Kim made a choking sound. But something in her eyes said her shock wasn't just over seeing a random shooting victim.

"You know that guy?" Ethan asked, a sick feeling settling in the pit of his stomach. "Was he the friend you came to visit?"

She stared at the medics pushing the gurney alongside the house to the street. "His name is Blake Owens. He used to be a resident at Hope Manor."

"Do you know why someone might want him dead?"

Her head turned slowly from side to side, and then came to an abrupt stop.

"Kim?"

"No. I don't know." She swallowed. Hard. As if she was trying to dislodge the boulder-size lie.

He'd been a cop long enough to spot them. But this wasn't the place to press her.

A police officer, winding crime-scene tape around the perimeter, glanced in their direction.

Ethan urged Kim to keep moving. He needed to find out what she was hiding before the police got ahold of her. They cut across the adjoining yard and slipped between the houses to the street. Police cruisers blocked both ends. Gawkers stood along the sidewalk. In the distance, thunder rumbled.

When Kim spotted the clutch of police officers questioning bystanders, she began to tremble.

But it was the sports car parked in front of the victim's house that caught Ethan's attention. Seeing no reason to sugarcoat the obvious, he said, "Blake was the friend you came to see. Wasn't he?"

She stopped next to a silver Ford Escort with flat tires he presumed was hers. "That's crazy."

"Is it? So the treads of that white Camaro up there won't match the tracks outside Hope Manor? Because in case you missed it, the back taillight is smashed."

Kim sucked in a breath. "Okay, yes, I recognized Blake's car this morning."

"So why not report him?"

"Because he used to be a resident. Something like that would've lost him his parole. I thought I'd talk to him instead. But then those vandals came along before I got the chance."

"You were going to *talk* to a guy who ran you down in broad daylight, and you're calling me crazy? What were you thinking?"

Her expression hardened. "I was thinking about the damage that rumors of a hit-and-run by a former resident would do to the manor. I don't expect you to understand. You've only been here a day. You couldn't possibly care about the manor's survival the way I do."

He felt like dog meat. The woman was as loyal and compassionate as they came. How could he have suspected her of trying to protect a drug dealer?

He edged her out of view of the cops. The ambulance wailed to life, a glaring reminder of the danger she was in. He had a bad feeling that someone didn't want Blake to talk to her. And with a bullet in his head, the kid wasn't going to give Ethan an explanation anytime soon.

"I'm sorry, Kim. I was out of line. Believe me, I want to help you." More importantly, he wanted to get her out of here before the police connected her—or him—to the shooting. "Come on." He nudged her toward the house that backed onto his. "I'll drive you home."

"What about the vandals? The police will want their description."

Ethan held her in place. The last thing he needed was a cop unraveling his cover. So far, other than the officer on the perimeter tape, no one had paid them any attention. "Since you're parked nearby, the police will record your license plate, and stop by your house in due course."

"But if I leave without talking to them, won't that make them suspicious?"

"Not once they see the condition of your ankle."

In the meantime, he needed descriptions of the punks, because chances were good one of them shot Blake, or saw who did. And Ethan needed to talk to them before the wrong cop got to them. Or to Kim.

Witnesses in this case had a bad habit of showing up dead.

A news truck squealed around the corner and stopped at the end of the street.

Great, just what she'd hoped to avoid by not reporting Blake in the first place.

Ethan tilted his head, and waited for her to meet his gaze. "Let me drive you home?"

The compassion in his eyes tugged at her heart. Twice in one day he'd come to her rescue. Why not make it three? "Okay."

He deftly skirted her around the officers canvassing the neighborhood and the reporter charging toward the scene, and led her back the way they'd come.

What would the police think if they found out she'd fled? Then again, if she admitted why she was in the area, some ambitious reporter was bound to find a nosy neighbor who'd identify Darryl's truck as being here, too. He'd squealed away minutes before the shot was fired. But people's memories had a bad habit of getting those kinds of important details confused. Or they'd theorize he snuck back. She could see the headline now—Former Hope Manor Resident Shot By Founder's Son.

Everyone who knew Darryl knew how protective he'd become of her since Nate had stomped all over her heart.

She misstepped, turning her ankle on the uneven pavement.

Ethan's strong arm circled her waist, unleashing a flurry of butterflies that made her feel as if she'd tumbled into the middle of a Jane Austen romance novel. She allowed herself to lean on him, borrow the strength and protection he offered. Just for a little while.

He was so different from Nate. Ethan took immediate, confident action, where Nate was indecisive and slow to respond.

A pang of guilt squeezed her chest. She wasn't being completely honest with Ethan.

He steered her between two houses, practically carrying her to spare her from putting too much weight on her ankle, and her guilt increased. Ethan had shown her nothing but kindness.

"The dark green Chev is mine," he said.

"How soon do you think the police will come by my house?"

"Hard to say. Sometime tonight. Tomorrow at the latest, unless they get a solid lead."

She shivered. If anyone had overheard Darryl threatening Blake, the police or reporters or both would dig up whatever incriminating information they could find on him—like that he'd been a regular at the gun club with his friend Frank. His friend who was now serving twenty years in a federal prison for manslaughter.

Oh, Lord, Darryl wouldn't shoot a kid just because he drove a little recklessly. He wouldn't. Please let Blake be okay. And please let the police track down the shooter quickly.

Ethan helped her into his car. The air inside was stifling. He cranked up the air-conditioning, and then glanced at the line of cars idling at the end of the street—employees from the candy factory, likely. "The police must be checking cars. Prop your injured foot on the dash. Let me do the talking."

Was it just her guilty conscience that made Ethan sound as though they were fugitives?

A few minutes later, a police officer wearing those mirrored sunglasses, whose chief purpose had to be to intimidate the person staring into them, stepped up to their window. "License and registration, please."

Ethan reached into the glove box, handed over his registration and then pulled his license from his wallet. "We heard a gunshot. Someone get hurt?"

The officer responded without emotion. "The victim's in critical condition."

Kim smothered a gasp.

Ethan shot her a silencing glare.

She buried her hands under her legs so the officer wouldn't catch her wringing them. If the police connected her to the car near Blake's house she'd look as suspicious as her brother. Maybe she should call Ginny and talk to her husband, Rick, about what happened. Reporting in, so to speak, before they came looking for her had to look better in the end. "My phone," she blurted, remembering that she'd dropped it when the shot rang out.

Ethan's silencing glare swept over her a second time.

"Why are you in the neighborhood?" the officer asked as he recorded the license information.

Ethan motioned to the row of duplexes. "I moved into 103, second floor apartment, on Saturday. Haven't had time to change my license yet."

"And the woman?"

"Kim Corbett."

"Relationship?"

"A friend," Ethan said, with a lilt that implied something more.

Kim's heart gave a funny kick.

"She hurt her ankle," Ethan explained. "I'm taking her to have it checked."

The officer wrote down everything Ethan said, and then looked at her. "Address?"

"Two-thirteen Maple Crescent."

His attention zeroed in on Ethan again. "Do you have any weapons in the vehicle?"

"No, sir."

The officer opened Ethan's door. "Could you step out of the car, please?"

Ethan turned off the ignition, his expression pained. "It's okay," he said to her before climbing out, but suddenly every warning her brother had ever voiced about her being too trusting screamed through her head.

She'd known this man less than twelve hours—twelve hours in which she'd been threatened twice. He lived in a seedy neighborhood and maybe carried a gun. And she'd just let him convince her to leave the scene of a crime!

If he was really an ex-cop like he said, why didn't he tell this guy? Play up the professional courtesy card?

Or was that why he was playing it by the book, not making waves?

Too trusting! The voice in her head screamed.

The officer patted Ethan down, glanced at the interior of the car and then said, "Do you mind if I look in your trunk?"

"Not at all. I've got nothing to hide," Ethan said easily, although Kim thought she glimpsed the muscle in his jaw flinch.

The officer riffled through the trunk, and then handed Ethan back his license and registration. "Thank you, sir. Have a good day."

Kim closed her eyes and let the air seep from her chest. He didn't have a gun. That was good, at least.

Ethan climbed in the car. "What were you saying about your phone?"

"I dropped it in the street." She lowered her voice. "When I heard the shot."

"Okay, we'll go back and find it." He rolled down the window again. "Officer, my friend dropped her phone. I need to turn around for a minute and see if we can find it."

"Go ahead." The officer backed up a few steps so Ethan had room to turn on the narrow street.

Kim pointed to a pothole a few yards past the factory's entrance. "I stumbled up there."

Ethan parked, then scouted the area in ever-widening sweeps. After what felt like hours, he returned, frowning. "I'm sorry. There's no sign of it."

Her throat went dry. She felt like gagging, and it wasn't from the sickly scent of gumdrops. "If those punks picked it up, they'll know my friends' numbers, my home number. With reverse lookup, they'll figure out my address." If they were brazen enough to chase her in broad daylight, who knew what they'd try under the cover of darkness?

Ethan slanted her a sideways look as he slid into the car beside her. "Why are you worried they'd come after you again?"

Her heart skipped as she realized that from his perspective there was no logical reason why they would. Why would they risk getting caught after they'd already gotten away?

She tried for a self-deprecating smile that felt weak even to her. "I guess because Dad drilled into our heads the importance of keeping our private information private. Residents will use anything as leverage to manipulate us."

He regarded her steadily, intelligence shining out of his chocolate-colored eyes, and she shifted on her seat. "Is that the only reason?"

Blake's ultimatum to her brother—*I go down, you go down*—flashed through her mind. She needed to talk to

Darryl, find out why he thought Blake had targeted her. Find out if he'd snuck back and shot him.

No, she couldn't ask him that. He'd be horrified that she'd think him capable. And she sure couldn't confide in Ethan that particular fear.

His fingers brushed past her cheek and gently pulled a leaf from her hair. "Kim, I want to help you. But unless you level with me, I may not be able to protect you."

She straightened. "I'm quite capable of taking care of myself."

Ethan arched his eyebrow.

"Okay, today was an exception. But nothing like this has ever happened to me before."

He started the car and nodded at the officer as they passed. "Skulk around in neighborhoods like this one and you're asking for trouble."

"That from a man who lives here," she said wryly.

"*That* from a man who doesn't want to see you hurt."

His words burrowed into her wounded heart and nestled there. She recalled his stricken expression when he'd knelt over her in the ditch. He'd feared the worst, and something told her he'd seen the worst before. And that the experience still haunted him. He looked at her now with a mixture of frustration and disappointment.

She dropped her gaze, fiddled with her shoelaces. "Take the next left to get to my street," she said, loosening the laces pinching her swollen foot. She tried not to wince at the way it throbbed.

Ethan jerked the steering wheel right.

"Where are you going? I said turn left."

"Not anywhere you're going to be happy about."

FIVE

Ethan flexed his fingers on the steering wheel, wishing for a fleeting second he could wrap them around her slender throat. "I'm taking you to the hospital," he growled. "Your ankle's swelling by the minute."

She slammed her foot to the floor. "It's fine."

"It's not fine. Look at it."

She did and frowned. "Okay, but my mom and Darryl will be worried about me."

"So call them."

"No phone, remember?"

He tossed her his.

She glanced at her watch and handed it back. "Never mind. Mom will still be at the hospital."

"Good, because so will we." Ethan stopped outside the E.R. doors and commandeered a wheelchair. Not that he hadn't enjoyed having her lean on him. That was the problem. He was here to do a job. Period.

Out of the car before he got to her door, she scowled at the chair. "I don't need that."

He wheeled behind her and bumped the chair against the back of her knees. "Sit." He leaned down to adjust the footrests, and a strawberry scent teased his nostrils. He'd always been partial to strawberries. He straightened quickly.

Noticing how good a suspect smelled was not in his job description.

A nurse wheeled Kim inside while Ethan parked.

He took the opportunity to phone the chief. "There's likely a connection between Blake's shooting and my investigation. I need you to keep me informed of any leads."

"So far, all they've got is a witness who saw a black truck screech away. What do you have?"

"I'm not sure yet." The ten-minute drive had netted him nothing more than a detailed description of the vandals and the strong impression that Kim was holding out on him. He couldn't recall hearing or seeing a getaway vehicle. But he'd been so focused on getting Kim to cover, all he'd been listening for was more gunfire. "I'll fill you in on the details later." Details he hoped he could wheedle out of Kim during the lengthy hospital wait. "In the meantime, if investigators bring in a couple of suspects—baggy pants, wiry builds, one with a pockmarked face—do me a favor and keep them alive."

"I don't like the sound of this."

"Neither do I." Ethan pocketed his phone, but when he stepped into the waiting room Kim was gone. He knocked on the glass separating the room from the admitting desk. "Excuse me. Has Kim Corbett been taken to an examining room?"

The receptionist glanced at the list on her clipboard. "Sorry, sir, she'll have to wait awhile yet. A nurse will come get her when an examining room is available."

Ethan squinted out the E.R. doors. He'd monitored his rearview mirror the entire drive. No one had followed them. But if the cop who had stopped them reported their names to someone dirty...

Ethan hunted down the nurse who'd brought Kim inside. "Do you know what happened to the woman in the wheelchair?"

"A technician took her to X-ray. Second floor. Follow the green arrows."

Ethan rushed toward the stairs. Anyone could yank on a lab coat and pose as a hospital tech. He scaled the stairs two at a time and beelined straight for the receptionist. "Kim Corbett. Is she here?" Turning from the counter, he hunched over to haul in a breath just as a technician wheeled Kim out of the X-ray room.

Relief slammed into him, followed by annoyance, which must've shown on his face, because Kim gave him an apologetic look. "You don't have to hang around here. I can catch a ride home with my mom."

"Of course I do," he said, feeling like a brute. After all, it wasn't her fault he was losing it. "As if I'd abandon you," he added, smiling at her. "You're stuck with me until I'm sure you're okay."

The pleasure that flickered across her face arrowed straight to his heart.

He took over steering her chair, cursing his inappropriate reactions.

"She goes back to the E.R.," the technician said.

Ethan wheeled her onto the elevator. A stocky, tattoo-plastered hippie stood in the back.

"Tony," Kim exclaimed to the fifty-something man. "What are you doing here?"

The man shifted uneasily. "I'm not feeling so hot." His gaze darted from Ethan to her elevated foot. "I heard you hurt your ankle. How is it?"

"I'll live."

Tony eyed Ethan suspiciously.

"Oh, I'm sorry," Kim said. "I forgot you haven't met Ethan yet. He's our newest staff member, and was kind enough to drive me here."

Mellowing, Tony thrust out his hand. "Good to have you on board."

What was with the man's sudden about-face? And how had he *heard* about Kim's ankle?

The elevator door swished open and Tony hurried out. "See you around."

Ethan wheeled Kim back to the E.R., where a nurse directed them to a private examining room equipped with splints and plaster.

Ethan closed the door after her. "Was that called-in-sick-today Tony?"

Kim chuckled. "Yes."

"How well do you know him?"

"I've known him since I was little. His size and the tattoos plastered down his arms used to intimidate me. But he relates well to the youth. Really well."

"They trust him?"

"Oh, yeah. He's a bit of an idol to some of them."

Tony sounded like the kind of guy who'd have no trouble recruiting kids to do his bidding. Ethan pulled up a chair in front of Kim's and, straddling the back, gave her a grave look. "Don't you find it strange that a guy who's never taken a sick day calls in minutes after the incident outside the manor? And, hours later, shows up at the hospital the same time the driver arrives with a gunshot wound?"

Kim's jaw dropped. "What are you suggesting?"

"A guy almost runs you down. Then when you go to see him, you get chased by a couple of vandals, and he gets shot. I'm sorry, Kim. That doesn't sound like a coincidence to me."

She stared at him for a long minute. "You think Blake deliberately tried to hit me?"

"Or scare you, yes."

"That's crazy. I haven't seen Blake since he was released over a year ago. He never had a beef with me."

"Okay, so who does?"

"No one!"

"Are you sure? Because it looks to me like someone hired

Blake to hurt you, and then tried to take him out before he could reveal who."

"And you think that someone is Tony?" She let out a laugh. "This is Miller's Bay, not Toronto."

Ethan kneaded the muscles in the back of his neck, debating how much information he could safely dole out. "You've got to admit he looks the part."

"Tony has devoted his life to helping troubled kids. He'd never do anything illegal."

"He sports a gang tattoo that suggests otherwise."

"His past is no secret. He did his time."

"Everyone has secrets, Kim."

She crossed her arms. "Why are you so convinced someone's out to get me?"

"Because I think you're in more danger than you realize. And I want to know why."

She shook her head. "No, I don't believe it. Bad things happen. And today was my day."

A nurse peeked in the door. "Miss Corbett, there's an urgent call for you at the desk."

Kim's gaze flew to Ethan's. "Who knows I'm here?"

Ethan wheeled her to the phone, where, despite the noise of staff and paramedics rushing past, he couldn't mistake the frantic voice of her brother.

"Kim, are you all right?"

Ethan grinned. Had to like a guy who worried about his sister.

For some reason, Kim looked more annoyed than pleased by his concern. "I'm having my ankle X-rayed."

Darryl's voice dropped too low for Ethan to make out what he said next.

"Since when do you get so worked up over my being late?" Kim responded. She paused, listening. "Someone stole my car?" Another pause. "Oh, that. I'm sorry I worried you. I thought you'd be here visiting Dad."

"Didn't you hear me?" Darryl's voice blasted so loud Kim pulled the receiver from her ear. "Your tires were slashed!"

"Yes, I know." Kim cupped her hand over the receiver and lowered her voice. "I didn't report it because at the time the police were too busy looking for the shooter."

"Shooter? What shooter?"

"Blake's."

Silence for a full thirty seconds. Then Darryl said something that made Kim's eyes flash. Returning the phone to the nurse, she said to Ethan, "Apparently, I have a ride home."

He smothered a chuckle. "I'm glad to see your brother looks out for you."

"Yeah, a little too much sometimes."

Ethan disagreed, but kept the opinion to himself. It was reassuring to know that her brother would keep an eye on her. Wheeling her back to the examining room, Ethan told himself he was relieved. He was here to find the person recruiting residents to peddle drugs, not to be Kim's bodyguard.

Of course, she still had information that could help him. He was certain of it. He'd gotten what he could from her on the Tony and Blake front, but he still needed to figure out how Aaron fit in. And fast. Because, somehow, he didn't think her brother would be thrilled to find him hanging around.

Ethan shut the door. "How well do you know Aaron Sheppard?"

"Oh, no. Did Darryl give him a hard time again? I told him to stop doing that."

"So you and Aaron hang out together?" he probed.

"We're not a couple, if that's what you're asking."

"It's not, but…" Ethan let his voice trail off. He'd been about to say he was glad to hear it, but that wasn't appropriate.

Or was it?

He hated to play on the attraction to gain information, but then again, lives were at stake. "I'm glad to hear it," he said aloud.

Her instant blush triggered a corresponding reaction in the region of his heart. He tried to ignore it. But after years of interviewing women too jaded to blush at much of anything, it was hard not to be charmed by Kim's involuntary response.

"So, why are you asking?"

He deals drugs! But if she couldn't think ill of a kid who drove his car at her, let alone a burly ex-gang member, she'd never believe it of clean-cut Aaron. "Just curious. Bad habit left over from my cop days, I guess."

Kim's expression softened. "Do you ever miss the job?"

He shrugged dismissively, but Kim persisted.

"Did something happen in Toronto? I mean…to make you want to give up police work?"

The compassion in her voice heightened his sense of guilt. Listing his "former" occupation on his Hope Manor job application had made him a shoo-in for the new position, but it was clear Kim wouldn't settle for his vague reason for leaving. He could tell her his cover story, but that would just heap on more guilt. And he couldn't tell her the truth.

"I'm sorry," Kim said. "I shouldn't have asked. It's none of my business."

"Not at all. You care. That's nice." He covered her hand with his—only to cement her trust, of course. But before he could congratulate himself on his detached professional behavior, his mouth opened and he heard himself say, "The truth is I was feeling restless and started praying for a new opportunity to open up. I wanted to do more. I wanted what I did to matter more. Then I got shot."

As Ethan recounted the shooting, Kim's heart wrenched. No wonder he was so paranoid about her safety. Between the sound of the gunshot and then seeing her hit the pavement, he must've relived that horrible day minute by minute. She cringed to think what memories the sterile white walls and cold marble floor of the examination room were stirring in him. "How long were you in the hospital?"

"Six weeks." His gaze shifted to the window. "It was another month before I was in any shape to do more than push papers."

"You never returned to active duty?"

The muscle in his jaw tightened, and for a moment he didn't answer. "For half a shift."

She gasped, imagining the worst. "What happened?"

"I lost my edge." He scrubbed his hand over his face and let out a weary sigh. "A doped-up break-in suspect waved a rifle in my face, and I froze."

"I'm sorry."

He straightened. "Don't be. God brought me here for a reason."

"Yes," she said, gratitude flowing through her. "I don't know what I would've done if you hadn't been here today."

The door burst open. Darryl stood at the entrance, his gaze sweeping from her to Ethan. *Just perfect.* Darryl took a step toward Ethan, eyes glaring with his unmistakable get-your-hands-off-my-sister scowl.

Thankfully, the doctor came in on Darryl's heels, cutting off her brother's inevitable tirade. The doctor snapped an X-ray onto the light board. "Good news is you don't have a break." He pulled up a stool and palpated the swollen tissue. "Looks like a slight sprain. With ice and rest you'll be back on your feet within a week."

"That's great news." Ethan stood as the doctor began wrapping a tensor bandage around her foot. "It looks like you're in good hands now." He pressed a note into her hand, and the warmth of his touch and quiet "call me" let loose the butterflies again.

Darryl opened the door for him and then glared at her over the doctor's head.

She glared right back. She had a few questions of her own

she wanted answered. Until she talked to him, she hadn't dared tell Ethan that her brother had been at Blake's.

The instant the doctor left with orders to stay off her feet for a few days, she hopped off the examining table and closed the door. Then she looked Darryl square in the eye and asked, "Did you shoot Blake Owens?"

"Me? How could you think such a thing?" he blurted, but the panic shadowing his eyes belied the pseudo-denial.

She poked a finger into his chest. "Because you were the last person who talked to him. Argued, actually. Threatened."

"You were there?"

"Yes."

"Then you know he was fine when I left."

"But did you come back?"

"No!" His shout rattled the cabinet doors. His voice dropped to a growl. "I told you to stay away from him. It'd be dangerous, I said. This ringing any bells?"

His face was crimson. She hadn't seen him this furious since he caught Nate two-timing her. And she wasn't sure she believed him. He was too overprotective for his own good.

A knock sounded on the door. And then a nurse handed Darryl a pair of crutches. "You can sign for these at the desk."

Handing the crutches to Kim, he motioned her toward the exit. "Let's go."

"We can't leave without visiting Dad."

"Right, of course," he muttered. His gaze darted from one hall to the next as he protectively shadowed her to the elevator. Instead of making her feel safe, his furtive moves scared her. Apparently, he was as worried as Ethan that someone was out to get her.

The doors opened and the hospital's palliative-care counselor greeted them with a look of concern. "What happened to you?"

"I sprained my ankle. Nothing serious." If she ignored Ethan's fear that someone was out to get her.

"Oh, that's a relief. Going up to see your dad?" The fifty-something wheelchair-bound woman was as sweet as her name—Joy. Whenever she visited Dad, she asked lots of questions about Hope Manor, which, of course, never failed to lift his spirits.

"How's Dad doing today? Have you seen him?" Kim asked.

"Yes. He was in good spirits, but…" Joy hesitated. "A gentleman stopped in. At first, your dad didn't appear to recognize the man, but then he became quite agitated and asked me to leave." Joy wheeled out of the elevator. "I'm relieved to know you're heading there. I was going to find your mom."

"She isn't with him?"

"I spelled her off so she'd go to the cafeteria and get some supper." A twinkle lit Joy's eyes. "She can't live on muffins alone."

Kim chuckled. Mom's habit of baking when stressed had kept the cancer ward well supplied with muffins.

Darryl rushed Kim into the elevator. "Come on. I don't like the sound of this."

"What's going on? Do you know who this guy is?"

Darryl punched the button for the fourth floor. "How am I supposed to know that?" he grunted, but the nervous bounce in his stance shouted definite suspicions.

"I don't know," she said sarcastically. "You seem to know a lot of things you're not telling me. Like why did you think Blake would bother me again?"

The blood drained from Darryl's face. "I—"

The elevator doors whisked open, cutting off the explanation.

An elderly couple joined them in the elevator for the rest of its climb to the fourth floor, leaving Kim to worry over the meaning of Darryl's pasty complexion.

"We'll talk about this later," he hissed as he maneuvered past the couple. Then he strode ahead, every line of his body rigid.

A powerfully built, silver-haired gentleman wearing an expensive suit and self-satisfied smirk stepped out of their father's room and breezed past Darryl without seeming to notice him. As Darryl turned to scrutinize him, the man gave her the kind of patronizing nod she imagined an aristocrat might deign to bestow upon one of his subjects.

By the time she glanced back to Darryl, he'd disappeared into their dad's room.

Kim wavered at the doorway. Brightly colored flowers from church friends filled every surface. Their fragrance mercifully banished the institutional odor, but they couldn't mask the rhythmic rasp of Dad's oxygen machine or the pallor of his translucent skin. He'd lost so much weight that his once-round cheeks had become sad-looking hollows.

Pained by the sight, she turned away and tried to picture how he looked before the cancer, but instead of an image of her healthy father, one of Ethan lying in a hospital bed recovering from a gunshot wound rose in her mind.

She rested her head against the door frame and drew in a deep breath. Why was she thinking about Ethan when she'd come here to see Dad?

"Kim," Dad exclaimed and promptly started coughing. The strain of the effort turned his pale complexion pink.

Kim propped her crutches against the wall and hopped to his side. She gave him a kiss on his papery cheek and then held his water straw to his mouth.

He took only a sip before pushing it away. "You hurt your ankle," he said, breathlessly. His eyes slipped shut. Fluttered open.

Kim straightened his bedsheets, wishing the pain meds didn't make him so sleepy all the time. "I'm fine."

Darryl squeezed her arm and whispered close to her ear, "I need to talk to Mom. I'll be right back." He was out the door before she could ask why.

Dad patted her hand. "Tell me about this new man the manor hired."

"His name is Ethan, and he seems passionate about wanting to make a difference."

"Glad to hear it." Dad glanced at the oxygen machine next to his bed and she could read his unspoken *I wish I could* in his eyes.

"Dad, your vision for Hope Manor won't be forgotten. You know that, right?"

With his eyes shut, he shook his head.

"Dad, I promise you, we'll carry on your work."

"It's not that." His fingers worried the edge of his blanket.

Kim sat next to his bed and cradled his hand between hers. "What's bothering you? Is it the man who just left?"

"No—" He choked on the word and broke into a coughing fit. With each inhalation, his chest rasped louder.

"It's okay, Dad. Try to take deep breaths." She offered him water, but he couldn't stop coughing long enough to swallow. The heart machine readout fluctuated wildly. She yanked on the call bell.

Tara, Dad's favorite nurse, rushed into the room. She checked his airway and listened to his breathing, but Dad grew more and more agitated.

Kim watched helplessly as Tara injected a needle into his IV.

A few moments later, Dad's eyes fluttered shut, and Tara tucked the sheets around him. She gave Kim a sympathetic look. "Perhaps you should let your father rest now."

Kim kissed his cheek. "I'll be back to see you tomorrow, Dad," she said, then quietly shut the door behind her. Focused on straightening her crutches, she turned straight into Aaron.

He caught her upper arms. "Whoa, there."

"Oh! Sorry. I didn't see you."

Still holding her, he smiled. "I'm not complaining. I'd hoped to find you here."

She scanned the empty hall looking for Darryl. "Why? Is something wrong?"

"No. Why would anything be wrong?" He repositioned her crutch and gave her shoulder a gentle rub. "I stopped by your house to make sure you were okay."

"That's sweet of you." She couldn't remember him ever being quite so attentive, or maybe she'd just been too preoccupied to notice. Or maybe her awareness of Ethan's solicitousness drew it to her attention. "The doctor said my ankle's sprained. I need to stay off my feet for a couple of days."

Aaron matched her awkward gait down the hall. "And how's your dad this evening?"

"A little unsettled." She snuck a sideways glance at Aaron. Muscle-bound, blond, tanned, he was quite good-looking, in a youthful, beach-bum sort of way. He cared about her father, went to church, helped with the young people's group, had a steady job. Exactly the kind of guy any girl would be thrilled to have on her arm.

So why didn't her stomach turn somersaults over his attention as it had with Ethan's?

Oh, brother, less than eight hours ago she'd insisted to Ginny that she didn't have time to date, and now she was obsessing over a little intestinal gymnastics. Or lack thereof.

She shook the notion from her head. "Did you happen to see Darryl on your way up?"

"No, sorry. Did you need a lift home?"

"That's okay. Darryl said he'd be right back."

"Are you sure? Because I'd be happy to drive you."

Suddenly, Aaron's attentiveness felt a little too…cloying. "That's okay, really. My brother will be looking for me."

Aaron's attention flicked past her shoulder, and alarm skittered across his face. "Okay, then, if you're sure. Take as much time off as you need to rest that ankle," he said. Then, turning abruptly, he disappeared out the stairwell door.

Kim turned to see what had prompted Aaron's sudden departure.

Two uniformed officers bore down on her.

SIX

Ethan shrank into the shadowy alcove opposite the hospital stairs. He itched to follow Aaron Sheppard, but he couldn't be sure the pair of cops flanking Kim's mom weren't on the drug ring's payroll, too.

When he'd spotted Sheppard's Mini Cooper swerving into the hospital parking lot, he'd worried the manor's interim director was up to no good, and he'd trailed him inside. Sheppard had skirted immediately to the back of the building and charged up the stairs to the cancer ward. Clearly, he frequented the ailing director's bedside often.

Not unreasonable, considering Sheppard was the dying man's replacement.

Then again, Ethan couldn't discount the possibility that the drug ring's infiltration went right to the top.

The prospect set his teeth on edge. If her father was part of a drug ring, Kim and her brother couldn't possibly be ignorant of the fact.

And where was Darryl, anyway? He was supposed to be protecting Kim.

"Here's my daughter," Mrs. Corbett said to the officers as she reached Kim's side. She fussed over Kim's ankle and Darryl's news about the car until one of the officers cleared his throat. She patted Kim's arm. "I'll be in with your father, dear."

The two officers—no distinguishing features, average height, average build, short dark hair—frowned at Kim.

Ethan couldn't see her face from his vantage point, but her white-knuckled grip on her crutches betrayed her nervousness.

One officer wrote furiously in a small black notepad as Kim responded to their questions, but the stony expression of the interrogating officer betrayed nothing.

The officer's gaze flicked to her leg.

She must've told him about being chased by the vandals. If those boys picked up her phone and located her house as she feared, he didn't want to think about what they might do to her next. Ethan had hoped to find them before the police. Not that he had a clue where to begin looking.

Kim's shoulder muscle flinched in response to a question. Ethan prayed they weren't baiting her. They grilled her with question after question as if she were a suspect rather than a victim. He supposed from their perspective that was a reasonable assumption. But he didn't have to like it.

"Is Blake going to be okay?" Ethan heard her ask, before her voice faltered.

Ethan knew her concern was genuine. But the officer ignored her question.

"A black truck was noticed fleeing the scene around the time of the shooting," the man said. "Did you happen to see the driver?"

Ethan leaned forward, watched her over the top of the magazine he held, feeling like a spy in a B-grade movie. She hadn't told him about a truck, but from the way her fingers flexed then tightened around the grip of her crutch, she'd seen one, all right. What else had she neglected to tell him?

After a long pause, she said, "I do remember a truck. But it left *before* the shooting."

The officer's eyes narrowed. "Are you certain about that?"

"Yes," she said adamantly.

A little *too* adamantly.

The suspicious glint in the officer's eyes suggested he'd noticed, too. But "Okay" was all he said.

The other officer flipped the notebook shut. "We'll be in touch if we have any more questions. You can pick up your car from the impoundment lot tomorrow."

Kim nodded.

The men sauntered around the corner, but Kim's mom joined her before Ethan could reveal his presence.

"Our ride's here," her mother said, and Kim's arms went rigid, her fists white.

"Where's he been?" she hissed.

"Running an errand." Mrs. Corbett rested a hand on Kim's shoulder. "Are you okay?"

"Yes, let's just go."

Interesting.

As they moved toward the elevator, Ethan slipped into the stairwell, then raced to the lobby. He watched them step off the elevator and followed at a discreet distance. They exited through the side door, where a black truck idled at the curb.

A bitter taste coated Ethan's throat. Kim may not have seen the driver outside Blake's house, but she knew who he was.

Her brother.

Okay, time to take the gloves off. If Kim didn't trust him enough to tell him the whole truth, she needed to know he'd figure it out one way or the other.

The moment Kim and her mom climbed into the cab, Ethan rounded the front of the truck and yanked open Darryl's door. "Were you at Blake Owens's house this afternoon?" he asked, point blank, scrutinizing Darryl's involuntary responses for signs of deception.

"What business is that of yours?"

"Ethan, what are you doing?" Kim asked, her tone panicked.

Ethan stopped the rejoinder he'd been about to utter. It was a good question. What *was* he doing?

He took a breath, regained his composure. Here he was,

standing in the middle of a public parking lot demanding answers from three potential suspects. *Real professional.* He couldn't have picked a better way to blow his cover if he'd tried.

"Who is this young man?" Mrs. Corbett demanded.

"Ethan Reed," Darryl ground out from between clenched teeth. "He works at the manor."

Yeah, and being there, being thrown back into his past, had to be what was throwing him off his game.

"I'll explain later," Kim said, shushing her mom's questions as she climbed out of the truck. She tugged him aside. "What are you doing here?"

"Watching your back," Ethan growled.

Her eyes widened. Then her look of surprise softened to an appreciation that rasped at the edges of his annoyance.

"Why didn't you tell me your brother was there?" he demanded.

Her eyes flashed. "Let me see." She tapped her finger to her cheek in mock contemplation. "Maybe because I knew you'd think the worst. Maybe because I wasn't about to snitch on my brother before I knew what really happened. *Maybe* because I've known you less than a day!"

He let out a puff of air. "Okay, but hiding information from the cops will land you in more trouble than you want, Kim. Believe me."

"Darryl left before the shooting. Don't you think I would've run to his truck if he'd still been there when those vandals started chasing me?"

"So why not tell the police?"

"Because they would've thought I was covering for him. Just like you did."

"What was I supposed to think? You didn't give me all the facts."

"If the police find out Darryl was there—and why—they won't bother looking for anyone else."

Ethan had to admit she had a point. Darryl had motive and opportunity. His prints were in the house. The police would nail him.

"And the press will crucify Hope Manor," Kim added.

"You could've told *me*."

"Now that you know, what will you tell the police?"

"Nothing. I don't want anything to happen to you any more than Darryl does." He searched her eyes for some sign of recognition that they could be on the same side. "Trust me."

Kim's gaze strayed to the staff-station window, where Ethan was supposed to be filling in the daily logs. Caught watching her, he gave her a lopsided smile and shrugged.

She looked away. He was proving to be much too big a distraction. She'd be better off focusing on her job instead of thinking about how his black polo shirt made him look tailored, yet strong, and a little bit mysterious in a dark-hero kind of way.

It was bad enough she'd had to spend three solid days with the man teaching him their protocols for handling issues with residents. Darryl could just as easily have done the classroom training.

She knew they'd just wanted her where they could keep an eye on her instead of home resting her ankle. And considering that her cell phone and the accompanying information were in the hands of who knew who, she should probably be grateful. Hanging out with someone as easy on the eyes as Ethan was certainly no hardship.

But the man was making her seriously lose her focus. Yesterday, while they were escorting two new residents to their rooms—Ethan in front, her behind—she'd been so busy noticing the cute cowlick at the back of his head that she'd failed to pick up on the animosity simmering between the two boys under their charge.

Even so, the instant the teen next to her lunged at the other one, she grabbed his arm and wrenched it behind his back. But the hundred-and-eighty-pound teen reared, slamming her against the wall. The blow made her see white.

He rammed her again, spouting some slur about people who interfered in gang business.

Ethan yanked him off her, and the next thing she knew four other staff were carting the pair away while Ethan crouched next to her on the floor saying, "Breathe."

Was it any wonder he felt like he had to watch her back?

He'd never believe she was usually one of the most capable, efficient workers on staff.

Back to regular duties today, she wandered to the foosball table where Curt and Melvin were getting loud. Moving into a resident's field of view tended to prompt him to tone it down.

With any luck, moving out of Ethan's would help her keep her mind on the job.

Through the staff station windows, Ethan watched Kim approach two residents playing foosball. Fifteen years after his own stint in a place like this, being on the opposite side of the glass felt a little surreal.

He ground the heels of his hands against his eyes. Between scouring the streets for the two punks who'd terrorized Kim and pursuing possible connections to his case, he'd gotten little sleep the past few nights. If only Blake would wake from his coma, maybe he could get some answers.

Ethan shook off his preoccupation with Kim and focused on the opportunity at hand. Darryl, the unit's third staff member, had been called to the gym to assist with an issue. With Kim busy, Ethan finally had a few moments of privacy to look over the resident logs. The two informants who were killed before they could finger their recruiter had both come from this unit. If he could detect any pattern between those who worked the unit prior to their releases, he might be able to pinpoint the most likely suspect.

He flipped back through the log's pages. Three staff members manned the unit at a time. Darryl, Tony and, up until recently, Mitch were the regular full-timers, while the part-timers tended to be college students who turned over faster than a dog with fleas. On several occasions like today, Kim, who normally worked unit one, had covered for another staff member. Of course, any staff member, from teachers to maintenance, could encounter the residents outside the units, whether in the classroom, the dining hall, the gym, the yard or the crafts rooms.

"What are you doing?" Darryl said sharply. The door thudded closed behind him.

Ethan's heart jumped, but he quickly recovered. "Familiarizing myself with the record-keeping."

"You can do that after the residents are confined to their rooms for the night. You're supposed to be on unit."

A sudden movement on the other side of the glass drew his attention to Kim.

"Take it easy," Kim said to the quarreling young men.

Instead of backing off, the larger of the two—a five-foot-ten, muscle-packed bully named Curt—moved in on the other kid, Beanpole.

Kim stepped between them as Curt took a swing.

Ethan flung open the staff station door and rushed the kid. But Kim ducked in time, and Beanpole's face took the brunt of Curt's blow.

Like lightning, Kim grabbed Curt's closest hand and twisted his arm behind his back. Ethan grabbed the other, barely restraining the urge to shove the kid face-first into the wall.

"You'll pay for this," Beanpole shouted, clamping his spurting nose. "This is assault. Your parole is screwed now."

Curt wrestled against their hold. "Beanpole started it."

"Move," Kim said, steering the kid toward the resident debriefing room.

Curt dug in his heels at the door. "Beanpole asked for it—I'm tellin' ya."

He was typical of the guys Ethan had been incarcerated with. Nothing was ever their fault.

Wrenching Curt's arm a fraction higher, Ethan shoved him into the barren room, then eased up. Took a deep breath. He'd lost it when he'd seen Curt's fist on a collision course with Kim's face.

And he couldn't afford to lose it.

He glanced at Kim. She hadn't hesitated a second to restrain Curt, despite the attack she'd suffered yesterday. *No thanks to him.*

"Ready to keep your hands to yourself?" Ethan asked in a carefully controlled voice.

"Yeah, okay," Curt said, sullen.

Ethan looked to Kim. "You want me to handle this?"

She released her hold and took a step back. "Sure. You've got to fly solo sometime. I'll watch."

He took another deep breath, debated what approach to take. If Curt was up for parole soon, he'd be just the kid the drug ring would want to recruit, if they hadn't already. And just the kid Ethan needed to win over to groom as an informant.

He slowly lowered Curt's arm. "What are you in for?"

Curt's rigid spine, the jut of his chin, exuded defiance. "I assaulted my old man."

Yeah, Ethan should've guessed. He knew this kind of kid. "Your dad must've made you really mad."

Curt shrugged.

"He used to smack you good before you got big enough to defend yourself, huh?"

Curt's face twisted into a bitter grimace, but his gaze dropped to the floor. "He never laid a hand on me."

No kidding? The teen was a dead ringer for an abuse victim. "How long have you been here?"

Another shrug.

"When do you get out?"

"Couple of weeks."

Mere weeks. Didn't give him much time. "I'm thinking this blowup wasn't about Beanpole at all. Am I right?"

Curt studied Ethan through narrowed eyes.

Kim retreated from the room, perhaps sensing Curt didn't appreciate the audience.

"Will you go home when you get out of here?"

"No." The ache in Curt's voice rooted into the darkest recesses of Ethan's heart.

Translation—*my parents don't want me.*

"So you'll be on your own." Ethan broke eye contact.

His gaze settled on the fist-sized dents texturing the walls. He winced, remembering the destruction he'd caused during his own stint in detention.

He turned his attention back to Curt. "I know how that feels."

"Yeah, right."

Ethan sighed. He recognized the defiance for what it was—a way to keep from being hurt. His own dad had visited him exactly once in youth jail, for a grand total of five minutes—just long enough to disown him.

Of course, he'd deserved his parents' rejection. Was that how Curt felt, too?

"I'm serious," he told the kid, hoping to spark some sense of connection. "When I was your age, my dad told me I was dead to him, but I figured I deserved it."

Curt snorted. "I don't give a crap what my old man thinks."

Ethan restrained himself from reacting. The kid had been soft-pedaled for the past eleven months; clearly, the approach hadn't worked with him. Maybe it was time to try a different tactic. Because if Curt stuck with his hard-nosed attitude, he'd never make anything of himself.

Ethan flicked a glance at the cameras monitoring the room and wondered if Kim was still watching. He turned his back to the cameras and lowered his voice. "I'll tell you something. I was in juvie for fourteen months. I didn't want to be there any more than you do. So when someone believed in me and gave me a chance to make something of myself, I took it. But I lived day in and day out with kids who'd never let anyone in. Kids like you. And you know what? Their lives amounted to squat."

Curt shrugged.

The sound of a throat clearing drew their attention to the door.

Terrific. How much had she heard?

Kim pierced Ethan with a laser-hot glare. "May I have a word with you?"

"Can it wait?"

"No."

He joined her in the hall and she laid into him faster than a police dog on attack. "What do you think you're doing?"

"Getting this kid to face what's *really* chewing his insides."

"He clobbered a guy because he beat him at foosball."

"If you think that kid cares one iota that Beanpole beat him at foosball, you're in the wrong job."

Kim's cheeks flamed. "I know there's more to it, but—"

"Curt has a chip on his shoulder bigger than Alcatraz, and it's going to get him in a lot worse trouble when he gets out of here if we don't make him face it now."

"But you don't do that by telling someone they're going to amount to squat. Curt's not stupid. You can't dupe him with reverse psychology. These kids know all the angles. Besides, probably all Curt's heard his whole life is that he'll never amount to anything. Do you seriously think hearing the same thing from you will motivate him to change?"

Ethan slid a glance to the room. He'd have settled for kinship, scoring a few points for shared experiences, winning a little trust. Changing the kid was Kim's department. His was to turn off the tap supplying Miller's Bay with a steady stream of drug pushers.

He shrugged. Maybe Kim was right. He'd been in Curt's shoes. And the tactic hadn't worked on him, either.

Kim's gaze turned warm and approving. She gave his upper arm an encouraging squeeze. "Be the one who believes in him."

The confidence shining in her eyes that he could be that person melted his resistance. *Oh, wow.* If more kids had someone like Kim championing them, keeping them off the streets, his job would be a whole lot easier. Something about her relentless defense of these troublemakers drew him in a way he couldn't ignore.

More than once in the past few days, he'd let himself wonder what it would be like to be loved by such a woman.

He plowed his hands through his hair. Okay, any minute his common sense would return. He'd lied to her, made her believe he wasn't a cop anymore. Worse, he'd agreed to help her save Hope Manor when he was supposed to uncover a scheme that would likely destroy it.

What was he supposed to do now?

SEVEN

Kim clutched her stomach and slumped onto a bench in the staff locker room.

"You okay?" Tony asked.

"You know how I am. I always feel sick after having to restrain a resident. I'll replay the situation in my mind for a week." At least she'd talked Mel out of pressing charges.

Tony gave her a wry grin. "It's the heaps of paperwork we have to do after an intervention that make me sick."

Kim laughed, remembering Ethan's identical complaint. She'd watched him debriefing Curt long enough to assure herself that he'd softened his approach. His claim that he'd served time in youth jail had piqued her curiosity, but she hadn't exactly been able to ask him about it when she confronted him over his interrogation tactics.

At first she'd thought his story might've been a ploy to get Curt to open up, but Ethan's empathy for the teen seemed too genuine. She hoped it was, because she couldn't condone lying, no matter how altruistic the reason.

Lockers clattered around her as the rest of the day shift prepared to go home. Tony pulled on his ball cap and sauntered toward her. "Aren't you heading home?"

"I'm waiting for Ethan. We're going to interview some former residents."

"What?" Tony tore off his cap and slapped it against his leg. "Why would you do that?"

"I'm gathering success stories for a newspaper article to boost the manor's image." She squinted up at him. Ethan's suspicions of Tony flashed through her thoughts, but she quickly reined in her runaway imagination. "Perhaps you could suggest someone."

Ethan stepped into the locker room at that moment and leveled a cautionary glare at her.

Tony replaced his cap and tugged the brim low over his eyes. "I suggest you think of another plan. Youth records are sealed. Former residents won't appreciate you hunting them down."

"I'm hardly—"

"Tony has a good point," Ethan interjected. "We may want to rethink your strategy."

Kim opened her mouth to argue. But one look at Ethan's tight expression made her swallow her protest.

"Yeah," Tony said. "Why borrow trouble?"

Ethan clapped his back. "Don't worry. Trouble is exactly what I'm trying to keep Kim out of."

Tony laughed. "Good luck with that. I've known her since she was knee-high. Trust me, keeping Kim out of trouble is a full-time job."

Kim folded her arms over her chest. "News flash, I'm standing right here!"

The twinkle in Tony's eye said *You know I'm right,* but he just chuckled and walked out, leaving her feeling like a little girl—the little girl who had accidentally handcuffed herself to Dad's office chair, only to be found by Tony.

"It's bad enough I have to listen to my brother take a strip out of me without Tony treating me like a kid, too. And you! You agreed we'd meet with ex-residents. Why'd you side with Tony?" The former residents she planned to visit had all remained in touch with the manor. If their stories could help, she was sure they'd be happy to share them.

"Because I didn't want him to know our plans." Ethan opened his locker and grabbed his wallet, keys and cell phone. "What did your brother say to get you all riled?"

Kim dragged her voice down a notch. "He chewed me out for stepping between the boys."

"He cares about you." Ethan's smile slipped. "That's a good thing."

His faraway look made Kim wonder if Ethan felt as though he had no one who cared about him. She was reminded of his comment to Curt about not being welcomed home. "Your family's not close?"

"I'm on my own."

"No brothers or sisters?"

"Nope." Ethan coaxed her toward the exit with a light touch to the small of her back that momentarily derailed her train of thought.

Of course, maybe that had been Ethan's intention. From his monosyllabic answers, he clearly didn't like talking about himself, which made her all the more curious. "What about your parents?"

Ethan held open the door and waited for her to step outside. "Why all the questions?"

"Oh, I've barely begun," she teased, giving his collar a tweak. "You know all about me, and I know so little about you. Except that you apparently spent fourteen months in detention."

His brief smile looked more like a wince.

"So the story is true. What were you in for?"

The door closed behind them with a thud, and the gray clouds overhead matched the bleak look in Ethan's eyes. "I'd rather not talk about it. It's not something I'm proud of."

"But you've overcome your past. That's the kind of success story I need to find for Hope Manor."

"I hate to tell you this, but I'm the exception."

"That's not true."

"Trust me, as a cop, most of my arrests were of repeat offenders. The routine gets pretty frustrating after a while."

"So what made the difference in your life?"

Before he could answer the question, her new cell phone regaled them with the upbeat ringtone she'd selected.

Ethan arched a brow. "Beethoven's Ninth?"

Pulling her phone from her purse, she shot him a surprised look.

Ethan grinned. "What? You don't think I got culture?"

She stifled a laugh as she answered the phone.

"Honey, you need to get to the hospital right away." Mom's words wiped the smile off her face.

"What's happened?" Kim flashed Ethan a panicked look and hurried toward the car.

"Hospital?" Ethan said, sliding into the driver's seat, and she gave him a terse nod.

Halfway to the hospital, she disconnected. It took another couple of blocks before she managed to swallow the despair lodged in her throat and fill Ethan in. "Dad stopped breathing. They've put him on a respirator." Raindrops, like tears from heaven, splashed on the windshield. She clenched her jaw against a rush of pain. "Please hurry."

Ethan reached across the seat and squeezed her hand. "Almost there."

His caring touch unraveled her. She wasn't ready to lose Dad. Not yet. Not ever. She closed her eyes against a swell of tears and prayed for strength.

Minutes later, Ethan pulled up to the parking attendant's booth and fished through his pocket for change.

She opened the door. "I'll run from here. Thanks for the ride."

"Kim, wait."

"There's no time." She hurried toward the building, dimly

registering Ethan telling the parking attendant to keep the change. She sped around the corner of the building to grab the side-entrance door.

A car door slammed, and the slap of shoes on wet pavement quickened toward her.

Thinking it was Ethan, she flung a glance over her shoulder.

The pockmarked teen she'd seen vandalizing her car lunged at her, shouting slurs. He caught hold of her purse as she grabbed for the door.

Letting her purse rip from her shoulder, she yanked open the door and slammed hard into a solid wall of muscle.

Powerful hands caught her by the arms. "Get out of here!" the man barked at her attacker.

"This ain't your business, old man," the kid snarled.

"Yeah, it is," the well-dressed man shot back with a tone that dared the kid to defy him. "Now, drop the purse and git."

The kid *got,* and Kim's breath swooshed from her chest. "Thank you," she whispered, stunned, and looked into her rescuer's face for the first time.

He smiled kindly.

She smothered a gasp. "You're Dad's visitor from the other night," she stuttered, taking an instinctive step back.

His fingers tightened around her arm. "Wait."

She swallowed, forced herself to look at him. He'd just saved her from being robbed, maybe worse. So why was her heart pounding out of her chest?

Ethan parked in the first empty spot he could find and jumped out of the car to follow Kim into the hospital. His phone bleated.

"Reed," Ethan barked into the phone.

"We've got another suspicious OD," Chief Hanson said without preamble.

Stifling a curse, Ethan glanced at the building, then slid back into his car, out of the rain.

"The victim had a Hope Manor card in his wallet," the chief continued. "The kind with the helpline number the staff hand the kids when they're released. This kid—Greg Sawyer—got out less than a month ago. His card wasn't even dog-eared yet."

Ethan groaned. This solidified their theory that the kids were being set-up to sell drugs from the moment they left the manor. If only he'd been able to convince Curt to trust him, maybe he'd have a name.

"Ecstasy pills were scattered over the kid's night table, but between you and me, the doc noticed an injection site next to one of the kid's piercings."

"I don't get it. Why would they take him out?"

"Sawyer's mom came to the station to report his suspicious activities. Looks like the drug ring decided to silence the kid before we could get to him. Make it look like an overdose."

"He's dead?"

"As good as. They took him to Memorial. But it doesn't look like he'll regain consciousness. Clearly, I've got a leak in my department. And the message is clear. You mess with them, you pay. You'll want to watch your back."

"I hear you." No one in the department was supposed to know the chief hired him for this operation, but that didn't make it so. Ethan pocketed his phone and prayed for the boy, a victim of his own greed perhaps, certainly his own stupidity. If only they could've convinced him there was a better way to live. But fat chance of that happening when one of the very staff members who should've pointed the way recruited him into a drug ring.

Ethan's thoughts turned to Kim. She'd be heartbroken to learn about Greg. Not that he was free to tell her. That would have to wait until the information went public. Which, considering her father's downturn, was just as well. Ethan scrubbed his hand over his face. People were being silenced left and right, and he was no closer to identifying the guy behind the orders.

A white sports car whipped past and out of the lot.

The sight of a pockmarked teen at the wheel made Ethan's already knotted stomach lurch. The kid fit the description of Kim's vandal. What was he doing here?

Ethan stuffed his key in the ignition and chased after him. One brake light blipped at the corner. Blake's car?

Caught by a red light, Ethan slapped the steering wheel in frustration. He was going to lose the kid. The light turned green, and he veered around the three cars ahead of him to take the corner. The sports car was nowhere in sight. Ethan cruised the street, checking parking lots. Seeing nothing, he sped back to the hospital and snagged a parking spot near the side door.

As he stepped out of the car, Beethoven's Ninth sounded from the direction of the flower bed.

Ethan frowned. His gaze arced over the rain-drenched buds.

Another ring sounded.

Aha, there. He scooped up the phone, tamping down a rising panic. Where was Kim?

He scanned the grounds, absorbing every detail, every indentation that might indicate what happened—chewed up grass, scuffs in the gravel, something.

But there was nothing.

Kim was a fighter. If she'd been attacked, there'd be some evidence of a struggle.

Ethan yanked open the hospital door and scaled the stairs two at a time to her dad's floor. Striding down the hall, he glanced in every room. At room twelve, he stopped.

Kim sat inside, head bowed over the bed of a frail old man. Safe.

Ethan slid her phone into his jacket pocket, his heartbeat finally slowing to a normal rhythm. Had she simply dropped it?

Now that he'd found her, he stood, uncertain, outside the

door, not wanting to intrude. Strangled breaths rattled her father's chest, and Kim winced with each inhalation.

Ethan found himself wincing in turn, gripped by a sudden, almost irresistible desire to wrap his arms around her and offer what comfort he could.

Except he didn't belong here. She needed the comfort of a man who would stand by her through the months of grief ahead. A man worthy of her affection.

Not a man whose mission would blow apart everything she was straining to hold together.

His chest ached, and in that moment he realized he'd gotten too close. He'd known her only a few short days. Yet, there it was. Too close.

The best thing he could do for her was walk away. Walk away from her, and walk away from this case. But walking away wasn't an option. The drug ring needed to be stopped before another innocent victim got caught in its noose.

"Ethan?" The voice came from the hallway.

He turned and a flood of emotions assaulted him. "Joy? What are you doing in Miller's Bay?"

"It is you!" Joy wheeled toward him, her ever-present smile ringing in her voice.

Old feelings of guilt balled in his throat. Scarcely lifting his gaze from the floor, he edged away from Mr. Corbett's door.

Thanks to his reckless driving, Joy had probably spent most of her life in one hospital or another, dealing with the consequences of the paralysis he'd caused. And not once had he scrounged up the courage to visit her. Bracing his hand on the wall, he forced himself to make eye contact.

To his surprise she wasn't dressed in a hospital gown. The lithe figure of the athlete she'd been had rounded into a grandmotherly one, but she looked stylish in a bright pink blazer over a black blouse. The badge pinned to her lapel said Counselor.

She touched it, a hint of pride in her eyes. "As you can see,

I work here. I moved to Miller's Bay a few years ago. What about you?"

"Oh, um." He waved toward Mr. Corbett's room. "I'm visiting a friend."

Joy wheeled closer and reached for his hand. "Come, sit a moment and tell me how you're doing."

Joy was a toucher. He remembered that about her. Maybe because in jail, contact had been prohibited. But the staff had always overlooked Joy's need to cover his hand with hers or give his arm a reassuring squeeze.

"I've been so worried about you ever since I read about the shooting. I pray for you every day," Joy said, clasping his hand the way he remembered.

Emotion clogged his throat and for a moment he didn't think he'd be able to reply. He swallowed. What did it say about him that the closest thing he had to family was the woman he'd put in a wheelchair?

She led him to the alcove. "I sent a card to the station for you. Did you get it?"

"Yes, thank you." He sank into a chair opposite her and hung his hands between his knees, suddenly ashamed that, aside from the letter he'd written Joy when he graduated from the police academy, he'd never sent her anything. "I'm sorry I haven't kept in touch."

"Oh, honey, I never expected you to. I know that seeing me in this chair is painful for you." She hesitated a moment. "But you have to know that God used my accident for good. Look at you. You've grown into a fine young man, out there fighting crime, making the streets safer."

Humbled by Joy's acceptance of her fate, Ethan bowed his head. Not once in all the times she'd visited him in detention had she blamed him for her condition. A staff member who knew Joy once told him that she'd always been devout—although the first few months after the accident had been really hard for her. Then she'd heard about Ethan's guilt-ridden attempt to end his life, and helping him had become her new mission.

Looking back, he could see she'd practiced tough love. "If I can live without the use of my legs," she'd said, "I don't want to hear any more nonsense about you throwing away your life. You owe me more than that."

He owed her. The words had resonated in his mind, and he'd latched on to the chance to make things up to her.

"You are a new man in Christ," she'd told him, quoting from the Bible. "The old has gone. The new has come." And he'd done his best to live up to her belief in him.

Joy cleared her throat, pulling him from his thoughts. "Have you moved to Miller's Bay or are you just visiting?"

Ethan glanced down the hall to assure himself that no one was listening in. "I recently relocated here."

"Well, Toronto's loss is our gain." She patted his knee. "I imagine you needed a change of scenery after that hoodlum almost killed you."

He fidgeted. The last thing he wanted to do was disappoint this woman by telling her—for the sake of his cover—that he'd given up police work. "Yes, I guess you could say that."

Across the hall, the ice machine chomped into action, and then Kim appeared, carrying a glass of ice chips.

Ethan sprang to his feet. "Kim, is your father okay?"

"Oh, yes. Stable, anyway. For now. I'm sorry I—"

"It's okay," he gently cut short her apology. "I understand."

Her gaze shifted to Joy and back to him. "You two know each other?"

Reflexively, he stiffened. "Uh, yeah. Joy helped me through…um…some difficult circumstances a while back."

Joy smiled graciously, but shook her head. "The Lord did the work. I merely had the privilege of pointing Ethan in the right direction." She rested her hands on the wheels of her chair. "It was lovely to see you again, Ethan. I hope we can talk again soon."

Ethan stepped awkwardly out of Joy's way.

Kim cast an anxious glance toward her father's room.

"You go back to your dad," Ethan said softly. She was distressed enough. News of the punk's appearance could wait. "I just wanted to make sure you were okay."

"I am now, but…" Her bottom lip quivered, and she tugged it between her teeth. "That kid who vandalized my car was here."

"I thought so." Ethan tried not to let how much that worried him sound in his voice. He pulled her phone from his pocket. "I found this outside. Did the kid approach you?"

She thumbed a smudge of dirt off the screen. "He snatched my purse and would've made off with it if a passerby hadn't scared him away. I was so focused on getting to Dad I didn't see the kid coming at me until it was too late." She shuddered, and Ethan had to fight the urge to pull her into his arms.

"He didn't hurt you?"

"Just rattled me. I would've forgotten to pick up my purse if the kind man who rescued me hadn't stopped me."

"You're sure you're okay?" He scanned her from head to toe to satisfy himself.

"Yes." She turned the phone over in her hand. "I suppose I'd better put a call in to the officer who questioned me about the vandalism. I just don't understand why this kid has it in for *me*."

Neither did Ethan, but nothing was going to stop him from finding out.

EIGHT

At the sight of Aaron pulling away from Kim's house in that ridiculous Mini Cooper, Ethan's mood went from bad to worse.

The overdose victim hadn't regained consciousness by the time Ethan tried to see him last night, and Kim's purse snatcher had abandoned Blake's car at Harbor Park and then disappeared. So Ethan was no closer to figuring out who was behind the attacks on her, let alone whether they had anything to do with his case. He hoped she'd be up to doing the interviews, because he was counting on at least one of the former residents being able to identify whoever was recruiting the kids.

Now, spotting his prime suspect cavorting with Kim, the woman he'd come to think of more as a cohort in his investigation than a suspect, grated in his chest.

He parked on the street opposite her parents' home—an older two story in need of a coat of paint on its weathered wood siding. A majestic oak shaded the driveway, and a wide veranda spanned the front of the house. Ethan grabbed the two cups of coffee he'd picked up and crossed the street. The soft purple hues of early morning had burned off, and the piercing sunlight that emerged promised another scorcher.

As he drew closer to the front porch, he noticed Kim sitting on a swing in the corner, her knees pulled to her chest, her head bowed, her cascading hair concealing her face. He set the cups on the step. "Kim, are you okay?"

She lifted her head, her face pale, her eyes red-rimmed.

"Hey, what's wrong?" He hunkered down in front of her and reached for her hands. "Is it your dad?"

A whisper of a smile trembled over her lips as she shook her head. "Aaron just told me that Greg Sawyer, one of the residents I was a primary worker for, died this morning. Overdosed."

Ethan started at the news. The chief hadn't notified him of the boy's death. "I'm so sorry."

"I can't believe it. He seemed like a kid who would turn his life around." A tear leaked from her eye, and she swiped at it with the back of her hand. "I thought, if he was having trouble, he'd call. I told him to call anytime."

"This isn't your fault." Ethan tucked her hair behind her ear, wishing he could do more. "The boy chose his own way," he said softly.

Kim squeezed her eyes shut and nodded.

A tear splashed onto Ethan's hand, making his heart ache. Her compassion for the residents in her care went beyond anything he'd ever experienced. She deserved the same support. Never mind that he shouldn't be the one to offer it, that he'd already let himself get too close. For now, he could do this for her.

He wrapped her in his arms and cradled her head against his chest, trying not to notice how silken her hair felt spilling through his fingers, and how perfectly she fit into his embrace.

"Shh," he whispered, wishing he could tell her everything would be okay. But a boy was dead. There was nothing okay about that. How he wished he could've spared her another loss. How he wished so many things could be different.

After a long while Kim drew in a deep breath and stiffened as if bracing herself. She quickly pulled her arms from around him and leaned back, her gaze skittering every which way but at him. She cleared her throat. "I'm sorry for crying all over you. I don't know what came over me. Between almost losing Dad last night and now this…" She swallowed, swiped her sleeve across her damp cheeks. "I'm sorry."

He rose, took a step back. "You have nothing to apologize for."

He'd deal with his own regrets later.

"Thank you," she said, her voice steadier. "I'm okay now."

Good. If only he were.

"Um, what brings you by?" she asked, offering a tentative smile.

He gave his head a mental shake and refocused on his original mission. He retrieved the coffees he'd brought and, handing her one, joined her on the porch swing. "I thought we might do those interviews. If you feel up to it."

Peeling back the coffee's plastic cap, she let out a small sigh. "I don't think we should now."

A stray hair caught on her lips and he checked the motion to brush it aside. He had a job to do, he reminded himself. And at the moment his job was to expedite these interviews. "Working on your article, knowing you're doing some good trying to save the manor will help. Don't you think?"

"I'm not so sure."

He took a sip of coffee, giving her a moment to reconsider, not wanting to push, despite how desperately he needed some fresh leads. When she showed no signs of breaking the silence, he couldn't bring himself to ratchet up the pressure. "I understand. The interviews can wait."

"No, I mean, I'm not sure we should do them at all. Darryl is right. We shouldn't draw any more attention to Hope Manor."

Terrific. Great time for her to start listening to her brother. "But your article idea would be positive attention."

"No, you don't understand. Any mention of the funding cuts is bound to stir a ruckus. Greg's death would become front-page news, instead of being buried in the middle of the paper where most people won't read it." Kim rubbed her fingertips over her forehead, started to say something then stopped herself. "The thing is, Greg's isn't the first overdose death in town. In the past six months, two other former residents died in a similar way."

"I see," he said, as if it was the first he'd heard of it. "That link will certainly work against us."

"Yeah, what if the police blame the manor for the growing drug problem?"

"Do you think it's to blame?"

"Of course not!" Her shoulders dropped in defeat. "But this doesn't look good for us."

Wasn't that the understatement of the year? With a push of his foot he set the porch swing in motion and let his gaze travel over the quiet street. "In the short time I've been at the manor, our routine searches have turned up three stashes of drugs. Clearly, a number of residents have a problem. How are they accessing the drugs?"

"Visitors sometimes slip them past our searches. It happens. What concerns me more is, the police told Aaron that Greg was selling. Greg came to Hope Manor on mischief charges and he leaves a pusher?" Kim worried the lid of her coffee cup. "I'm afraid that one of the longer-serving residents is setting kids up with outside connections."

"Could be." Encouraged that she'd trusted him enough to voice her suspicions, he ventured a second theory. "Or it could be an employee. Seems to me an employee could get away more easily with slipping drugs inside."

"No way," Kim shot back with an adamancy that made him lift an eyebrow. "All our employees are carefully screened."

"The police may see it differently."

She released a heavy sigh. "That's what I'm afraid of. If they're investigating the manor, the government will never change its mind about funding."

Kim's transparency about what was going on confirmed Ethan's belief in her noncomplicity.

Her expression turned suddenly hopeful. "You must have some inside connections. Can you find out if the police are investigating the manor?"

"I don't think trawling the police department is a good idea," he said, hating the disappointment his refusal brought to her eyes. "Questions might spark their curiosity."

Ethan finished his coffee in one last gulp. Obviously inactivity didn't sit any better with Kim than it did with him. And now that he was confident she'd only withheld information to safeguard the manor's reputation, there was no reason why she couldn't help. If he could get her to scrutinize the other employees' actions more closely, she might notice unusual behavior he missed. "We'll just have to do our own sleuthing."

Kim had always considered herself adept at getting residents to open up to her, but by Monday evening, her attempts at sleuthing had amounted to squat. She straightened and re-straightened the shelves in the manor's cramped library as she waited for Curt to choose a book. Talking wasn't permitted in the library, and the pervasive silence sucked her thoughts into a downward spiral. Could an employee—not a resident—really be responsible for the drug problem?

Curt waved a Western novel in front of her face. "I'm ready."

He was a voracious reader, not something she saw too often among male teens. She liked to encourage residents to read, to think beyond their narrow world and dream about possibilities, because possibilities gave them hope. And hope was what they desperately needed. "Tell me," she said, as she escorted him back to the unit. "If you could live anywhere in the world, where would you choose?"

"The Prairies."

"Really?"

"Sure. It's got lots of wide-open spaces. You can see for miles."

"Ah." Since he'd been locked in this facility for the better part of a year, she could see the appeal.

Returning to the unit, they found Ethan and Melvin watching the Discovery Channel.

"Hey, Curt," Ethan said. "Did you want that rematch in Ping-Pong now?"

"Yeah, sure." Curt tossed his book onto the nearest table and waited for Ethan to get the paddles and ball from the locked cupboard.

Ethan's attitude toward the kids had done an about-face since last week's incident with Curt. Ethan had a knack for drawing the teens out of their shells. Kim liked how he made a point of sitting down and talking with each one. The kids reveled in his company, and she couldn't blame them.

She did, too.

When Ethan had shown up on her doorstep Saturday morning and comforted her over Greg's death, she hadn't wanted him to let go. The steady beat of his heart beneath her ear and the shelter of his embrace had given her a peace she hadn't felt in a long time—a sense that everything would truly be okay.

And his eyes…

He'd looked at her as if he wished with all his heart he could take away her grief. No one had ever looked at her like that before.

Curt sliced a return shot, and Ethan missed the ball entirely. His good-natured laughter filled the room and wrapped around her, filling her with a sense of happiness.

Ooh, boy. She needed to get a grip. She worked with him day in and day out. Not the kind of guy she wanted to entertain dating for one of her infamous two-week stints. Not to mention, Ginny didn't need any more fodder for her little pep talks.

The nine o'clock bell dinged. "Okay, guys, time to get ready for bed," she announced.

"Three more minutes," Curt pleaded, whacking the ball across the table. "I've almost got him beat."

Ethan grinned and tipped the ball over the net, evening the score. "Don't be so sure."

"Aaah," Curt groaned. "That doesn't count. Kim distracted me."

"You snooze, you lose."

The rest of the boys returned from the computer room under the escort of Leon, one of the college part-timers, and the group gathered around the Ping-Pong table.

"Come on, Curt, clobber him," Jake yelled.

"No, nail him, Ethan," Matt countered. "Or Curt's head won't fit through the door."

Seeing the camaraderie and enthusiasm of the boys, Kim felt as if her heart might burst.

"Game point," Ethan called, serving the ball.

They rallied the ball back and forth more than a dozen times to the cheers of their spectators. Then Curt sliced one to the corner of the table, and Ethan missed.

Not that anyone would know from his grin. His gaze met Kim's across the table, and his wink momentarily jolted her heart out of rhythm. "Good game, Curt. Now time for bed."

A chorus of groans met the news, but the boys dutifully made their way to their lockers. Forty-five minutes later, they were locked in their bedrooms, and Leon checked out for the night.

Kim collapsed into a chair in the staff station.

Ethan tossed her a can of pop from the fridge. "Gotta like the night shift. Play hard for a few hours then ship them off to bed."

"We're not done yet. We still have to fill in the logs. Then, if we're lucky, we won't get a string of requests for the bathroom, and we'll have a chance to finish reviewing the files before the first perimeter check."

"Curt is the next resident scheduled for parole," Ethan said. "I'm hoping to win his trust enough that he'll open up to me if someone approaches him with a proposition."

Kim cringed at how calculated that sounded. "He seems to really like you, and that's saying something. Kids come here hardened and defensive. They typically resist trusting because life has taught them that it's safer to keep their distance."

"According to his file, his mother took the beatings likely intended for him." He studied the condensation dripping down the side of his pop can. "My guess is that he's got a whole lot of guilt pent up inside of him."

"That, and the assault that landed him here was the result of finally defending his mom. But afterward, his mom sided with her husband's version of events."

He grimaced. "Yeah, I saw the same thing as a cop all the time. The victim doesn't trust the system to protect them, so they protect their abuser to avoid further punishment."

Kim let out a weary sigh. "His mom's lie must've felt like the ultimate betrayal."

"The way I see it, unless Curt admits that he blames himself for his dad's attacks and for not doing more to protect his mom, we can't help him confront them for the lies they are."

"You sound like you've had some personal experience with this."

Ethan's gaze shuttered.

He'd reacted the same way when she had happened upon him with Joy at the hospital. "Why don't you like to talk about yourself?"

The hum of the overhead fluorescents grew deafening.

Ethan set down his pop can and snagged a resident's file from the shelf. "There are far more interesting topics, and we have more important things to do if we're going to figure out who's luring these kids into the drug world."

Okay, so he didn't even want to talk about why he didn't want to talk about himself. She could take a hint. She jittered her pen between two fingers and pretended to scan the log. "Darryl got upset when I told him what we think is going on."

Ethan spun toward her, crushing the file folder in his tightening fist. "You told him what we're doing?"

"Of course."

He slapped the folder on the desk and paced the room. "Have you told anyone else?"

"No."

"Good. Don't. The last thing we want to do is drive the guy underground."

"You can't think that my brother would be involved in such a thing!"

He stopped and faced her. "Rule number one in an investigation is *no one* is above suspicion."

She crossed her arms over her chest. "Not even me?"

He gripped the armrests of her chair, his gaze dark and brooding.

She instinctively drew back, and then caught herself. No, she refused to be intimidated. She tilted her head at a defiant angle. "Is that the best you got?"

Amusement flickered in his eyes, and then…something else. *Oh.* Her stomach turned flips. Pathetic-crush flips. His lips were awfully close.…

For a frozen instant, neither of them moved. Then a smile whispered across those lips. Time seemed to stop. The room grew so quiet, she could've heard herself breathe if she hadn't been holding her breath.

A thousand emotions swirled in Ethan's eyes—a chaos of *shouldn't*s and *want-to*s that made her wonder if her little crush wasn't so very pathetic after all.

He straightened, and she fought back disappointment at his abrupt withdrawal.

"No," he said, answering the question she'd forgotten she asked. "I believe you are as innocent as they come."

Not as innocent as he thought if the crazy skipping of her pulse was anything to go by.

She'd wanted him to kiss her.

So why didn't you kiss him?

Coward.

Yeah, he'd messed up, Ethan thought for the umpteenth time in the past four days.

Ethan unlocked the unit's laundry room door. What had he been thinking?

He might as well have written *I want to kiss you* across his forehead. Or better yet, *Idiot.*

Only, he could've sworn he'd seen the same interest flare in her eyes as had flashed over him. Good thing he hadn't acted on it or he would've really gotten burned.

He could handle the crazy shifts he'd been banished to since that night. Ethan glanced at the afternoon sun slanting through the bars on the windows and stifled a yawn. Shifts that never overlapped Kim's. One guess who'd made that request.

Ethan headed back to the common area.

"You have to stand at the door of the laundry room until Matt's done," Darryl barked. "Inmates tend to chug down anything for a high they can get their hands on, including detergent."

Yuck. Ethan took up his post, keeping one eye on Matt and the other on Darryl. Maybe Kim hadn't been the one who'd requested the schedule changes. Her brother clearly didn't appreciate his interest in her. Sure, he'd claimed that Aaron always changed up the schedule on the new guys to familiarize them with the different routines, but after four shifts that "happened" to be during Kim's off hours, Ethan knew someone had ulterior motives.

At least he'd made some headway in earning the confidence

of a few of the boys, Curt included. Not that he was any closer to narrowing in on a prime suspect. Tony watched him like a hawk. But nothing in Tony's actions suggested he wanted to lure the boys into joining a drug ring. Aaron was harder to figure out.

Kim had shown zero awareness of Aaron's illegal activities, if accepting drugs from a group of youths and tossing them into a Dumpster could be considered illegal. The guy's record was squeaky-clean. But his latent interest in Kim…

Ethan didn't want to think about why that irked him so much. Instead, he once again let the image of Kim's expression after he'd caught hold of her chair play across his mind. It had been bad enough when the startled look in her eyes changed to one of teasing challenge, but when her gaze had dropped to his lips and her strawberry scent had wafted up to him, he'd been hard-pressed to remember where he was and why it would be a colossally stupid move to kiss her.

"Hey, man, you hear me?"

Ethan shook the thought from his head and turned his attention to the kid trying to elbow his way past with an armload of laundry. Ethan checked the pile for contraband and locked the laundry room behind them. Next, he unlocked the kid's personal locker, so he could store his stuff out of reach of the other residents.

Ethan checked his watch. Ten minutes to changeover. He'd finally coaxed Kim to interview a few ex-residents with him. She'd sounded almost eager.

"I said—" Matt's voice rose as if he were talking to a hard-of-hearing grandfather "—you can lock it."

Ethan's attention snapped to the kid. He locked the box and escorted Matt back to the common area. He should be grateful he'd spooked Kim into avoiding him most of the week. Just thinking about her seriously affected his concentration.

Twenty minutes later Ethan emerged from the building to find Kim waiting for him.

He couldn't stop the smile from spreading across his face, but he quickly reined it in.

Then Aaron eyed them from his office window, and Ethan threw restraint to the wind, placing his hand at the small of Kim's back.

He felt a surge of satisfaction as the other man turned away.

NINE

Kim tensed at Ethan's touch. Not because the warm pressure bothered her, quite the opposite. His touch uncorked a cascade of bubbly, bursty feelings in her stomach. A lighter-than-air, walk-on-clouds feeling. The kind of feeling that had once whisked her to fairy-tale dreams of happily ever afters.

And that was the rub. If she'd felt this way toward Nate—the two-timing lowlife who'd duped her for months—clearly, her feelings couldn't be trusted.

"You okay?" Ethan asked, guiding her toward his car.

"Yes. Sorry. My mind went somewhere else for a second."

"Hey, Kim, hold up," Aaron called from behind them.

Kim turned, causing Ethan's hand to drop away. The cool air that rushed into its place made her shiver. Or maybe it was the icy glare Aaron speared at Ethan as he turned.

"Ginny mentioned you were giving a talk to the youth group Thursday night," Aaron said, focusing a warmer gaze on her. "I'd be happy to help."

Kim swallowed her surprise. "Yeah, sure, that would be great."

"I thought we might get together tonight to discuss ideas."

Kim snuck a peek at Ethan's face. "Um, I can't tonight." In addition to interviewing former residents, she hoped to coax Ethan into talking about himself. If her heart was so determined to trip over him, she should know more about the guy.

Sure, he was caring, attentive, protective, not to mention great with the kids, but everyone had a skeleton in their closet.

"What's the topic of the presentation?" Ethan asked.

Aaron looked him up and down. "Saying no to drugs."

"Our youth pastor asked if I'd talk about the dangers of drug use," Kim explained, recounting his concerns about a couple of the kids.

"Sounds important," Ethan said. "Why doesn't Aaron join us for a quick bite now, and the two of you can work out your presentation before we tackle those interviews?"

Kim looked at him, dumbfounded. She'd obviously read more into his gentle hand at her back than he'd intended.

But Aaron held up his palms. "That's okay. It can wait until tomorrow."

"Yes, let's plan on tomorrow," Kim said.

Aaron shot Ethan a smirk and then sauntered to his car, whistling a tune.

Ethan snorted. "The guy's falling all over himself to get you to go out with him."

"You think?" Who could trust what men seemed to want? After all, Nate had seemed to want her right up until he ran off with her roommate.

Ethan ignored her flippant question. "Is Ginny in the habit of mentioning your plans to Aaron?"

Kim shrugged, then gave her ponytail a toss and climbed into the car. "Maybe she thinks Aaron would be a good catch."

"You think?" Ethan mimicked, sliding into the driver's seat. "How well do you know him? Has he ever used drugs?"

"Aaron?" Kim laughed. "He's as by-the-book as they come. He's so honest he once drove twenty kilometers to return money to a scrap-metal recycler who overpaid him."

"He told you that?"

"No, one of the kids who helped him collect the scrap told me."

"Does Aaron hang out with them a lot?"

She turned to face him. "Aaron's not recruiting kids into a drug ring, if that's what you're getting at."

"We have to consider all the possibilities."

She rolled her eyes. "Right." She pulled out the sheet of paper with the names and addresses of the three former residents who'd agreed to talk to her.

Ethan glanced at the first address and started his car. "Do you think some of the church teens might be using?"

"I don't know. I don't know them that well."

"If any do, it would help if you could find out who they buy from."

"The likelihood he'd be connected to the resident recruiting pushers would be slim. Don't you think?"

"In a town this size, the pushers are all gonna be cogs of the same wheel. And I think we need to seriously consider that the one working the manor is an employee, not a resident."

"Surely you're not suggesting Aaron, because he—"

"Not Aaron." Ethan glanced at the rearview mirror and made a sudden left turn.

Kim braced her hand on the dash. "What are you doing?"

"Tony has been following us since we left the manor."

Kim twisted sideways to peer over her seat. After a week of double-checking her surroundings every other second for signs of her purse snatcher, she couldn't believe she hadn't noticed the black pickup that swerved onto the road behind them. "I can't see the driver."

Ethan flicked on his right turn signal and coasted to a stop in front of a strawberry stand.

The driver sped past, cap pulled low over his eyes.

"Are you sure that was Tony?"

"No doubt."

Kim squinted after the truck. "There's got to be a reasonable explanation."

"Yeah, Tony doesn't want us to contact former residents. And I can think of only one reason why. And you're not going to like it."

Ethan waited another minute before pulling back onto the road. The stench of chicken barns filtered through the car vents, and up ahead, he noticed something else that smelled rank—a black pickup half-hidden behind a hedgerow.

He lifted his foot from the accelerator. "Looks like we've got company again."

Kim looked to where he pointed. "This is ridiculous. Let's just confront him. I'm sure a simple conversation will sort this out."

Ethan let the car slow to a crawl. "What makes you think we can believe Tony's explanation?"

"He's a terrible liar. I've seen him play board games with the kids. He can't bluff worth a hoot."

"It may be easy to tell if he's lying. The hard part is figuring out why."

"I don't see a better option. Do you?"

Ethan worked his jaw. He didn't mind a woman who challenged him—kind of liked it, in fact—but did she always have to be right? The last thing he wanted was to put her in any more danger. He parked a car length shy of Tony's position and motioned for Kim to stay put.

He might as well have tried to stop the wind.

"Why are you following us?" she blurted the instant Tony jumped out of the truck.

Tony moved in on her.

"Stay where you are," Ethan said, his tone low and dangerous. "And answer the lady's question."

Tony veered toward him. "You're the one who needs to answer the questions. You weren't on the job a day before you started making moves on the boss's daughter. What's your story?"

"He was *not* making moves on me," Kim protested. "Don't you think I have any sense at all?"

"Sure, but you're vulnerable right now. Some men—" he flashed Ethan a scowl befitting a cockroach "—like to take advantage of that."

"I would never take advantage of a woman." Ethan's throat constricted. When this was over, that's exactly how it would look.

"No? What do you call showing up at Kim's house on a Saturday morning with coffee?"

Kim gasped. "You were spying on me?"

"I'm watching out for you. Your brother asked me to keep an eye on you after that kid ran you down."

Kim's arms shot up, her gaze veering skyward. Then she muttered something incomprehensible before taking aim at Tony. "I am not made of glass. I am quite capable of looking out for myself."

Ethan couldn't help but admire her feisty attitude even though he didn't want to take that risk any more than Tony.

"Yeah, well, you know how Darryl is," Tony growled. "He has this wacky idea that someone paid Blake to scare you."

Kim paled. "Why would anyone want to scare me?" she demanded, but the crack in her voice betrayed the fear she'd been doggedly trying to ignore.

Ethan hugged her to his side. She'd been denying the deliberateness of Blake's attack for two weeks. Maybe she'd finally run out of rationalizations.

Tony looked pointedly at Ethan's hand on Kim's shoulder. "So that's how it is, is it?"

Kim slanted a glance at Ethan across the front seat of the car. He hadn't affirmed Tony's innuendo about their relationship, but he hadn't denied it, either. She could still feel the warm assurance of protection where his arm had circled her shoulders. Did he like the idea of them being a couple?

Did she?

What if it was just some macho, won't-back-down-for-nobody guy thing that had prompted him to pull her a little closer after Tony's pointed remark?

Ethan accelerated back onto the road and flipped down his visor against the reddening sun low on the horizon. "I think there might be some basis to your brother's concerns. Maybe this drug dealer thinks you know something."

"But I don't."

"Think. Have you seen anything recently that didn't seem quite right—an interaction, a conversation, a transaction?"

Her mind whirled back over the past few weeks, but the only interactions and conversations in her thoughts were those with Ethan. And what should that tell her?

"Kim?"

Jerked from her daydreaming, she realized he was waiting for an answer. "Oh, um…" She rolled down the window, but the hot flicks of air only tightened the muscles knotting the back of her neck. "No, I can't think of anything." She let her gaze drift over the gentle dips and rises of the passing farmland. Everything that'd happened to her coincided with Ethan's arrival.

Why had she never suspected him?

She shook the ridiculous thought from her head. From the moment she first looked into his eyes, she'd known she could trust him. She didn't know why. She just did.

"Could be you were threatened to ensure someone's cooperation."

"Cooperation to do what?"

"What do you think?" he said gently.

"I don't have a clue…" Kim felt the blood drain from her face. In its place crept a chilling numbness. "You mean, hurt Greg?"

"I was thinking more of recruiting kids to work for the drug ring."

"That's crazy. The person would just go to the cops."

"Unless he didn't think they could protect you." Ethan reached across the seat and squeezed her hand. "I want you to be extra careful until we figure this out. Okay?"

Finding it difficult to speak past the lump in her throat, Kim could only nod.

He stroked his thumb across her curled fingers, sending warmth spreading through her chest. "You know...contrary to what you might think, there are plenty of people who care about you."

Was Ethan one of them? she thought wistfully.

Or was this just his white-knight tendencies in action?

"People who could be coerced to do things for fear of your safety," Ethan continued.

He released her hand, and she buried it under her thigh, along with her fairy-tale thoughts.

"You have far too vivid an imagination," she said wryly.

"Tony would. Don't you think?"

"Tony?" Her voice rose with the absurdity of his suggestion. "Puh-lease, he'd take out anyone who threatened me. Not do their bidding."

"Good point. Then there's Aaron. He clearly likes you." Ethan returned his hand to the steering wheel. "He likes you a lot."

"Not enough to risk his career. Trust me."

"You never know." Ethan's gaze remained fixed on the road. "Love does funny things to a person."

Was that a hint of jealousy?

Heat flooded her cheeks. Yeah, in her dreams.

"We can't forget your brother," Ethan continued. "He'd likely do anything to protect you."

She laughed. "Believe me, if someone blackmailed Darryl, he'd go straight to Rick Gray—Ginny's cop husband. This is nothing but pure speculation, as ridiculous as Tony's assumption that we're a couple."

"But a blackmailer plays on a person's fear of going to the—What?" Ethan's gaze flicked to hers, then back to the road. "Tony thinks we're a couple?"

"Uh…" Ethan hadn't gotten that from Tony's remark? Her mind replayed Tony's comment and she winced at how far she'd let her thoughts get carried away.

"You know what I mean," she said, feigning nonchalance in the hopes that Ethan wouldn't clue in. "We didn't exactly put to rest Tony's allegations."

"Allegations? It's not as if we robbed a bank."

"I'd just like to know how you want to handle the innuendos."

Ethan laughed. "Oh…the innuendos. We can't have those." He pulled off the road at a bluff overlooking the lake.

"Why are you stopping?" The sound of the waves lapping to shore carried through the open windows with the sweet smell of lake air. Oh, great. Now he could focus his full attention on her idiocy instead of the road. "Go ahead, laugh it up, city boy. But rumors have a nasty tendency of spreading like wildfire in a small town."

"Wildfire, huh?"

"I'm serious." She swatted his arm. "Stop laughing at me."

He grinned unrepentantly. "I'm laughing with you."

"Do you see me laughing?" She reached out to swat him again, then gasped as he caught her hand.

Sudden awareness flared between them.

"I see…" Ethan cleared his throat. His gaze darkened and Kim's heart skipped a beat. "I see a woman so beautiful she takes my breath away."

He drew her closer, bringing her hand to his chest. The wild thrum of his heart pulsed through her, making her own heart skitter.

She drew in a breath. "Ethan, I think—"

"Don't," he whispered and brushed his lips over hers in the sweetest kiss ever.

A kiss that swept all qualms from her thoughts, and stole the last of her breath.

He leaned back just a whisper. "Wow."

"You can say that again."

He smiled. "Wow."

She swallowed, floundering for a witty response.

Ethan stroked her cheek. "I can see how that wildfire could get so out of control." He looked at her for a long, silent moment.

Wildfire? Oh, yeah, the rumors.

He started the car and pulled back onto the road. "We'd better get to those interviews."

Hmm. She touched her lips, reliving the kiss.

It hadn't been playful at all. It had been tentative and tender, as if he were holding back, afraid to give free rein to the emotions swirling in his eyes.

She'd never felt so moved. And amazingly, the realization didn't scare her.

For the first time since Nate, she wasn't breaking into hives at the thought of letting someone get close. Maybe the coward lectures she'd been giving herself for the past four days had finally sunk in.

I see a woman so beautiful she takes my breath away.

Ethan couldn't know the balm those unbidden words were to her heart, especially when he'd looked deep into her eyes as if looking beyond her appearance. With that look, he'd cut through the doubts Nate had left in his wake. She turned to the passing scenery. Everything about Ethan drew her in a way she'd never experienced. His teasing, his expressive eyes, even his protective concern that wasn't at all smothering like her brother's. And she was deeply grateful for his support in trying to save the manor.

It didn't hurt that he had those chocolate-brown eyes that made her knees go weak, or that his kiss melted her heart.

She turned her head to smile at him. His gaze was fixed on the road. His jaw looked carved from stone.

Her heart stuttered. Was he regretting their kiss?

Doubts gnawed at her throughout the evening.

Hours later, as Ethan drove her home, Kim looked for a softening in his features, some sign that the kiss they'd shared had meant something to him. Not once all evening had he brought it up. Not in the hours of interviews. Not during dinner. Not even now, with a thousand stars twinkling in the night sky.

Of course, it wasn't as if they could've sat around and gazed into each other's eyes while interviewing former residents. Not to mention Ethan had clearly been thinking more about ferreting out information on their resident drug pusher than gleaning examples for her newspaper article of how the former residents had turned their lives around.

It was her own fault for asking him in the first place to find out if the police were investigating a connection between the recent rash of drug crimes and the manor. She supposed once a cop, always a cop. And she couldn't help but admire his commitment to get to the bottom of whatever was going on, even if she was a little apprehensive about what it might do to the manor's reputation.

Yes, after the interviews, it had been perfectly understandable that he would stay stuck in detective mode, rehashing what they'd learned. She knew enough psychology to realize that a romantic lakeside restaurant was lost on a man locked in his problem-solving box.

Oh, brother, how much more pathetic could she get?

Now she was making excuses for him. If she hadn't seen the truth when Ethan declined the table tucked in a private corner of the restaurant in favor of one in the middle, she should've when the waiter came to light their candle and Ethan told him that wouldn't be necessary.

Considering how easily her heart had tumbled into his hands, she should probably be grateful for his reticence.

Her throat grew raw. She tugged her sweater against a sudden chill. Not so much a chill in the air as a chill in the atmosphere between them.

"Cold?" Ethan asked, and part of her wanted to say yes to see if he'd wrap his arm around her again.

Yup, she was pathetic.

"I'm fine. Thanks." Except suddenly, going home to an empty house was the last thing she wanted. She sat up straighter, squared her shoulders. "Would you mind dropping me off at the hospital? My mom won't be home yet, and Darryl has a meeting for something or other tonight. I'd like to see my dad, and this way I can give Mom a lift in her car."

Babbling. She was babbling!

"No problem," Ethan assured her, then lapsed into silence again.

She couldn't read his expression in the dim interior of the car. Maybe that was for the best, too.

He parked in front of the hospital. "Wait," he said, and walked around the car to her door.

She drew in a quick breath. Was he planning to give her a good-night kiss?

The way he barricaded himself behind the door as he opened it answered *that* question loud and clear. "When you leave with your mom, be sure to stick to the main entrance and the lighted sidewalks," he said. "Will Darryl be home by the time you get there?"

"I'll be fine, Ethan." She stepped from the car, feeling as though cement blocks weighted her legs.

He shifted, keeping the door squarely between them. "You need to be careful."

"If you're so worried," she snapped, more annoyed with herself than him, "maybe we should just tell the police everything."

"And ruin any hope of convincing the government to restore the manor's funding? No, let's just stick to the plan."

"Was the kiss in your plan?"

Ethan flinched, but said nothing.

Obviously not. She crushed her purse under her arm and moved to slam the door shut.

But Ethan held it firm. "Kim," he said, his voice agonizingly soft. He waited for her to meet his gaze. "I didn't plan for any of this to happen. The last thing I want to do is hurt you."

The street lamp's shadowy glow accentuated the regret creasing his brow.

Regret. *Right.* Because *I don't want to hurt you* was the line guys used just before they dumped a girl.

And technically, she wasn't even his girl.

"It's okay," she hurried to say, but even she could hear the hurt in her voice. "I understand. With all the talk of bad guys and the sound of the waves and... Well, we got carried away. I know I already regret—"

"Kim—" Ethan's rumbly voice rattled her bravado. He drew her around to his side of the car door and nudged it shut. Then he cupped her face in his sure hands and looked deep into her eyes with that knee-weakening gaze and brushed his thumb across her bottom lip. "I *don't* regret kissing you."

TEN

Thankfully, when she reached her dad's hospital room a while later, he didn't seem to pick up on the wide grin Kim found impossible to contain. Still on the ventilator, he was pretty unresponsive. She wasn't sure how much of the one-sided conversation he was following.

"Are you okay, dear?" Mom asked, returning from her late supper at the cafeteria. Her stooped shoulders and shadowed eyes betrayed the toll of her husband's prolonged illness.

"Yeah." She was more than okay. Ethan wanted to spend more time with her. "Um, I was telling Dad about the interviews for my article. Sammy—he's in college, can you believe it?—he gave me a great quote about how grateful he is for the faith Dad had in him when Sammy had none of his own."

Dad's eyes fluttered open, found Mom's and crinkled at the corners. His pleasure at the news warmed Kim's heart.

Ethan was so much like Dad in his interactions with the youth. Ethan had been amazing with the former residents they'd interviewed—genuinely empathetic, truly gifted at drawing out their stories and helping them recognize the positive changes in their lives. She could easily see herself falling for him.

Okay, okay. Maybe she'd already fallen just a tad.

Based on what she knew about him, anyway. If she was

going to go around kissing him, she wanted to know a lot more first. And she knew exactly who to ply for information.

"Mom, I need to talk to Joy for a few minutes. Don't leave without me, okay?"

"I'll be here."

Kim kissed her father's bristly cheek. "I love you, Dad. I'll see you later."

A pang of guilt caught her in the chest as she left the room. Her father was dying and everything he'd worked so hard to establish was at risk, and here she was getting giddy over a guy.

Not that Dad wouldn't want her to find someone special.

She didn't know who'd been more upset when Nate ended things, Dad or her. Of course, to Dad, Nate's about-face had been unfathomable.

Dad had always absolutely adored Mom. He liked to say that she'd saved him twice. First by pointing him to the Lord, and then by giving him her heart. And Mom's unswerving support of Dad's work—despite unpredictable hours—was an example Kim had aspired to.

"Kim, you okay?" Joy wheeled herself to where Kim had slouched against the wall outside the door.

"Hmm, yes. Just reminiscing. I'd like to talk to you, though, if you have a few minutes."

"Sure, is over there okay?" She motioned to the vacant chairs in the alcove.

"Yes." Kim perched on the edge of the closest chair, uncertain how to begin. "It's…um…about Ethan."

"He's okay, isn't he?"

"Yes, it's not that." She pictured how on-edge he'd seemed in this same spot not more than a week ago.

"Are you two dating?"

Her stomach fluttered at the mere suggestion. "I wouldn't call it dating, exactly." Dating never worked for her.

"Something's bothering you about him?"

"Well, yes. I really, *really* like him, and yet, I know so little about him. He doesn't like to talk about himself."

Joy nodded knowingly. "What has he told you?"

"About his police work and the shooting, and that he has no family, and that he was in juvenile detention."

"Did he tell you how we met?"

"You were his counselor, weren't you?"

"In a way. I'm so proud of how Ethan turned his life around after his time in detention. Guilt is one of the devil's favorite weapons."

"He wouldn't talk about why he was in custody."

The overhead lights dimmed. The PA system crackled, announcing the close of visiting hours.

"I figured he couldn't have done anything too bad," Kim rushed on. "Since he was able to become a cop, I mean."

Even so, imagining possible scenarios ramped up her heart rate. She really had no idea what kind of guy she was kissing.

"When Ethan's ready, he'll talk about that time."

"It's just that something's bothering him and I want to help, if I can."

"Be his friend."

Kim sighed. There had to be a way to coax Joy into sharing what she knew about Ethan without outright asking. "Be a friend, huh? Is that how you got over your accident? Through your husband's friendship?"

Joy's eyes warmed as they always did when she spoke of her husband. "No, I met my husband a number of years later."

"You radiate such a peace about life despite your challenges. How did you find that?"

"Not instantly or easily."

Frustrated by Joy's vague responses, Kim took a deep breath and went for broke. "Will you tell me why Ethan went to jail?"

Joy plopped her handbag onto her lap and rummaged through the outside pocket. "Ethan's story isn't mine to tell, but I will tell you how he helped me. The day he graduated from the police academy, he sent me this card." She pulled out a dog-eared greeting card with a picture of a bouquet of roses and the words *Thank you* printed in block letters on the front. "When I got this note, I was going through a very low time, thinking I wasn't much good to anybody, stuck in this chair.

"This letter changed all that. It reminded me that when I was helping Ethan work through his difficulties, mine hadn't mattered nearly so much. His note inspired me to start this counseling ministry. Now whenever the devil tries to make me think I'm useless to anyone I pull out Ethan's letter and reread it."

Joy lovingly stroked the picture on the front of the card. The color had faded from the many times she must've held the card in her hands, remembering the difference her faithfulness had made in one's man's life.

"Give him time," Joy said softly. "He's only been back to work for a couple of weeks. On top of the challenges of settling into a new police department, I suspect he's battling doubts and worrying about how he'll react the next time someone pulls a gun on him."

"Police department? Ethan doesn't work for the police. He works at Hope Manor. That's how we met."

Joy's eyes widened. "He does? I just assumed, I guess, but…"

A queasy feeling fingered Kim's stomach. Why would Ethan let Joy think he was still a cop?

"I was sure he was working on that teen overdose case. I saw him talking to the guard, and then he went into the boy's room."

"He was probably just visiting him. Greg was a former resident of Hope Manor."

Except Ethan hadn't known that.

Ethan hadn't been at the manor long enough to know that.

FREE Merchandise is 'in the Cards' for you!

Dear Reader,

We're giving away FREE MERCHANDISE!

Seriously, we'd like to reward you for reading this novel by giving you **FREE MERCHANDISE** worth over $20. And no purchase is necessary!

You see the Jack of Hearts sticker above? Paste that sticker in the box on the Free Merchandise Voucher inside. Return the Voucher promptly...and we'll send you valuable Free Merchandise!

Thanks again for reading one of our novels—and enjoy your Free Merchandise with our compliments!

Pam Powers

Pam Powers

P.S. Look inside to see what Free Merchandise is **"in the cards"** for you!

LIS-FM-12

W
e'd like to send you two free books to introduce you to the Love Inspired® Suspense series. These books are worth over $10, but they are yours to keep absolutely FREE! We'll even send you 2 wonderful surprise gifts. You can't lose!

REMEMBER: Your Free Merchandise, consisting of **2 Free Books** and **2 Free Gifts**, is worth over $20.00! No purchase is necessary, so please send for your Free Merchandise today.

Plus TWO FREE GIFTS!

We'll also send you two wonderful FREE GIFTS (worth about $10), in addition to your 2 Free Love Inspired® Suspense books!

Visit us at:
www.ReaderService.com

Kim's throat dried. When she told him about Greg, Ethan had acted as if the boy's death was news to him.

"Yes, that must be it," Joy said. Her gaze dropped to Ethan's card and a frown touched her lips. After a moment, she tucked the card back into her purse. "I'd better be getting home."

"Good night," Kim murmured as Joy turned and wheeled down the hall. Kim stared blankly after her.

What was Ethan doing in Greg Sawyer's hospital room the night he died?

Without opening his eyes, Ethan reached across the night table to snag his phone.

"Someone's on to you."

Ethan rubbed the sleep from his eyes and rolled out of bed. "Good morning to you, too, Chief."

"Switchboard just got a call for you."

"Did they happen to note the caller ID?"

"Blocked. Any idea who you might've tipped off?"

Ethan scraped a hand over his morning whiskers. "Could be Joy, the former acquaintance I told you about."

"Yeah? Well, don't count on the caller being someone who's on our side. I've got enough dead bodies on my hands."

The blunt remark jolted Ethan fully awake. Not that he ever worried for his own life. Kim's was another matter. If someone in the drug ring suspected he was a cop, anyone who appeared to be cooperating with him would be suspect.

He'd shocked himself as much as Kim when he kissed her. He'd tried to pull back, act professional, but when he'd seen how that hurt her, he couldn't remain aloof. Never mind that he hadn't planned on ever letting his heart get entangled with another woman. Not after his ex-girlfriend Stephanie had chewed up and spit out every last foolish notion he'd had that God might one day bless him with a woman to cherish.

When he'd asked Stephanie to marry him all those years ago, she'd said there were three people in their relationship—

him, her and his guilt. She'd said she couldn't live like that. But she'd merely confirmed what he'd known all along.

He didn't deserve her, or anyone. Not after what he'd done.

But somehow, Kim had burrowed under his defenses. More than her unwavering belief in the kids at the manor, her respect and pride in the ones who, like him, went on to make something of their lives had started to make him wonder if Stephanie was wrong.

Sure, he still lived with guilt. Anyone would.

And yeah, he probably didn't deserve a family after robbing Joy of her chance for one. But knowing he didn't deserve one hadn't quelled his longing for a woman to share his life with.

A woman like Kim. A woman who radiated God's love and mercy in everything she did.

His alarm clock buzzed, reminding him that he had to be at work in forty-five minutes. At least he had a short shift today. He'd been up until two in the morning trawling every haunt where drug deals were likely to go down.

He'd hit pay dirt at a beach party up at the lake.

The kids were too baked to care that answering his questions could dry up their supplies. Blake's name hadn't sparked recognition with any of the kids, but Greg's had. And Ethan had recognized two of the partiers from Aaron's rendezvous a couple of weeks back.

Except when he'd dropped Aaron's name, the kids had clammed up.

Ethan didn't know what to make of the reaction. A few minutes earlier, they'd been happy to tell him where he could buy all the crack he wanted.

Kim's brother's name had come up, too. Nothing definitive, but an angle worth pursuing.

And he shouldn't have any problem wangling an invitation to her home, given their kiss.

His conscience twanged.

After that kiss, Kim would believe that his interest in her

went deeper than wanting to help save the manor. He'd stepped over the line.

But the last thing he wanted to do was step back.

At least, the male side of him didn't. The cop side was telling him to cool things off before his emotions messed with his objectivity.

He groaned. *Too late for that.*

But he was beginning to think that Kim made him a better cop. Adopting her softer approach had certainly worked with Curt. If nothing else, the more time he spent with Kim, the easier time he'd have keeping her safe.

Yes, cultivating their budding romance was a win-win situation.

If Ethan thought a little kiss would blind her to what he was really doing in Miller's Bay, he'd better get used to disappointment, Kim thought. He'd pretended to be so moved by Greg's death, while for all she knew, he'd caused it. She should've known he was too good to be true. Most of this trouble had started after he'd shown up in town.

Well, she intended to figure out what he was hiding.

Using Dad's master key, Kim let herself into his Hope Manor office and set a cardboard box on the guest chair. The smell of dusty books and Old Spice transported her back to her childhood. She used to love to sit in the giant leather armchair, swinging her legs, her feet far from touching the floor. Dad would ask her about her day and tell her stories.

How she'd cherished the time Dad had spent with her, especially the talks they'd share over a good book. Kim drew the copy of *Charlotte's Web* from the floor-to-ceiling bookshelf that filled the east wall.

The story had been her favorite as a child, a picture of what Dad did for the kids in his care. And like Charlotte had done for Wilbur, Dad would try to help these kids to his dying breath.

Kim cleared the sudden lump in her throat. Now was not the time for reminiscing. She needed to figure out how Ethan knew Greg, and if their connection had anything to do with everything else going on around here. She dropped the book into the box and added a couple more for good measure. If anyone asked why she was here, she'd say to clear out Dad's things. After all, Aaron would soon want to take over the office that went with his job.

Next, she pulled Greg's file from the archives drawer, and then sat at the desk to comb through the documents. Greg had been a pretty good kid. From a middle-class home, he'd lived with both parents, even had a part-time job bussing tables until he was picked up for stealing a car. He'd lived in the Niagara area all his life, so the probability he'd crossed paths with a Toronto police officer was next to nil.

Undeterred, Kim fired up Dad's computer and retrieved Ethan's job application, police check and letters of reference. Not only had Ethan been the youngest member of the department to make detective, he'd received numerous commendations. Not the picture of an officer who'd snuff out a boy in a hospital bed.

Kim's gaze wandered to the window overlooking the exercise yard. Two part-time staff were playing basketball with a half dozen level-B kids. Practicing, no doubt, for their upcoming game with the church's youth group. The match was one of many innovations Dad had introduced to help the teens appreciate fun alternatives to hanging out on the streets.

Curt dribbled the basketball down the court and tipped the ball over the lip of the net. As the other team maneuvered to take control of the ball, Ethan joined the game. He feigned a move to the left, then rushed right and stole the ball from his unsuspecting opponent.

Kim walked to the window, afraid that trick was exactly the kind of move Ethan had pulled on her.

Ethan passed the ball to Curt, then stopped midcourt and

looked straight at her—or at least at the window. She shrank back, although he couldn't possibly see through the one-way glass.

Curt scored and gave Ethan a high five. He was doing a great job at drawing Curt out. How could she think he'd hurt Greg?

Because he'd acted as if he didn't know the boy, she reminded herself, and returned to the list of commendations she'd been reviewing. Ethan had done everything from jumping into a raging river to save a drowning child, to rushing into the line of fire to rescue a woman caught between warring street gangs. For the latter act of bravery, he'd gotten a medal and a bullet in the thigh.

Kim reflected on the times he'd come to her rescue. From what she could tell, the shooting hadn't affected Ethan as negatively as he'd claimed.

On his very first day, he'd rushed to her aid twice. Then, when Curt had taken a swing at her, Ethan had been the first one through the door—not the sign of a man who'd lost his edge. And from the way he'd noticed Tony following them, his instincts were as sharp as ever.

She pushed her chair back from the desk. This was getting her nowhere. What had she expected to find? Some telltale reason he'd snuff out Greg's life?

She shook her head. Like she'd told Joy, Ethan had likely overheard that Greg was a former resident. He might've already harbored suspicions of a connection between Hope Manor and the growing drug problem—the same suspicions she'd voiced the following morning.

Suspicions he'd been quick to run with.

Or...

She'd been thinking Joy was mistaken about Ethan moving here to work for the local P.D. But what if Joy was right?

Kim scrolled back through Ethan's résumé. He hadn't just

been a street cop. He'd been a detective. *A detective.* So...
maybe he *was* working for the local P.D. Undercover.

It explained everything. Why he'd formed an attachment
to her so quickly. Why he'd been uncomfortable around Joy...
afraid she might blow his cover. Why he went to see Greg.

Kim stared at the screen, a sick feeling welling in her throat.
He had to be undercover.

Not once had he acted shell-shocked—his reason for quitting.

He'd acted like a cop. And she hadn't questioned his behavior because he'd been a cop. From the first day, he'd lured
her into working with him, claimed he wanted to help her save
Hope Manor. What a fool she'd been. Hadn't she learned anything from Nate's betrayal?

Ethan had to be investigating the drug problem. And whatever he hoped to find wouldn't save Hope Manor.

It would destroy it.

The government would latch on to any excuse to shut down
the place. And here she'd confided in him, believing he wanted
to help her, believing he cared, believing...

What did it matter now? The drug trade had to be stopped.

She shut down the computer and picked up a photograph
of Dad cutting the ribbon at the opening of the manor's new
workshop. She traced his smile. He'd poured his heart and soul
into this place. They all had.

And she'd let him down.

*Oh, Lord, there's got to be another way to stop them. I can't
let Ethan destroy all the good Dad's done. I can't.*

She set the photo back on the desk and strode straight to
the exercise yard. The lunacy of confronting him here roared
in her ears even as she scanned the players on the basketball
court.

But Ethan was gone.

Then chaos erupted in the yard and all thoughts of confronting him flew out of her head.

ELEVEN

"**Y**ard, now!" Kim's call blasted over the walkie-talkie on Ethan's hip.

His blood went cold. Kim wasn't supposed to be in today.

Propelled by the thought of someone getting to her inside Hope Manor, he raced to the door. "You stay here," he barked to the college kid manning the unit with him, and then sprinted for the yard.

He jammed his key into the exit door lock, but it wouldn't budge. Through the narrow window he couldn't spot Kim in the clutch of boys circling something near the perimeter. Shouts knifed through the walls. The boys closed ranks as Ethan wrestled with the lock. He burst through the door and plowed through the mob, praying he wasn't too late.

Within the circle of jeering boys, Darryl and Tony hauled an arm-locked kid to his feet.

Ethan's gaze thrashed through the crowd. Spotting Kim, he exhaled and headed straight to her. "Are you all right?"

She jabbed his chest. "This is your fault."

He glanced at the kid Tony and Darryl were escorting inside. Didn't recognize him. "What is? What happened?"

"Cory tried to escape. Apparently ever since you scaled the fence the residents have dared the newbies to try." She turned to the kids standing around the yard. "Show's over, back to your game." To Ethan she said, "What were you thinking, jumping that fence?"

He shrugged. "You screamed. I did what had to be done."

"Did what had to be done, huh?" She barricaded herself behind crossed arms.

He offered a lopsided grin. "I couldn't wait to meet you."

"Oh, sure." Scowling, she planted her hands on her hips.

Not exactly the response he was hoping for. Last night, he'd replayed their kiss a hundred times and envisioned at least as many scenarios of how Kim might feel about it come morning.

Not one came close to this. "What's really bugging you?"

"Joy and I had a talk."

Oh, no. Ethan wanted to moan. Joy must've told Kim about the accident. No wonder she was steamed. "I'm sorry, I should've told you."

The look of disgust in Kim's eyes dug the guilt further into his chest. It was Stephanie all over again.

"Oh, buddy, you're gonna be a lot sorrier." Kim's gaze darted to the residents scuffing around the court and back to Ethan. "Follow me. Now," she said between gritted teeth and marched him inside. "We need to talk."

Talk? It hurt just to breathe.

Losing her respect ate at his very soul. "I'm sure Joy's depiction of the accident was thorough. What more do you expect me to say?" He felt as though he'd been drop-kicked.

Kim steered him toward her father's office. "You and I both know Greg's death was no accident."

"Greg?"

"Of course, Greg." Kim unlocked the door and motioned him inside.

Everything about the room felt gloomy. From the black-walnut bookcases and desk to the barred windows behind it. Steel-gray filing cabinets consumed the remaining wall space, like coldhearted tattletales who never forgot a single transgression.

"Joy saw you go into Greg's room." Kim's voice dropped to a hiss. "I know what you are. You used me."

Oh, this was worse than he'd thought. Much worse.

"I can explain. I heard—"

Kim's hand shot out, stopping him midsentence. "Are you or are you not working as an undercover cop? And don't you dare lie to me."

Ethan pressed his fingers to the vein pulsing painfully at his temple. He could concoct an explanation—one that might retain her cooperation and not blow his cover. But looking into her pure green eyes, Ethan couldn't bring himself to lie. He'd worked dozens of undercover gigs, so why couldn't he keep a secret from *this* woman?

Because when you're with her, you only want what's best for her.

And more than that—she'd made him believe he might actually be good enough for her, even with his ugly secrets. But if he let this masquerade continue, the damage would be irreparable.

He reached for her hands. Once she saw the situation from his point of view, she'd understand why he had to keep his identity a secret. "Yes. I'm working on a case."

For a long painful moment, she just stared at him. Then she yanked her hands from his. "Get out. You're fired."

"Kim, please, let me explain. I wanted to tell you."

She jerked open the office door and held out her palm. "I'll take your ID and keys."

Climbing out of his emotions, Ethan reached over her head and shoved the door closed. "You don't want to do this."

She drew herself up to her full five foot six inches. "Oh, believe me. I do."

"If you fire me, if you tell people what I am, you'll only

attract more scrutiny. Trust me, a quiet investigation of Hope Manor is far preferable to a public one."

"Trust you? *Trust you!* Like you haven't been lying to me from the minute we met?" Her eyes flashed. "How could you do this? You know how much I want to save this place, what it means to me."

The desperation in her voice shredded the last of his rationalizations. "I'm not here to destroy Hope Manor."

"As good as. You must've had a hearty laugh over how easily you charmed me into helping you."

"No, it's not like that at all. I care about you. If I didn't, I would've denied everything."

Her jaw worked back and forth, as if chewing over his explanation. Her fingers—clenched around the doorknob—turned white.

Covering her hand with his, he loosened her grip. Before he let her open the door, one way or another he needed her assurance that she wouldn't expose his mission. "The police chief thinks there's a dirty cop on the force. That's why he hired me to figure out who's recruiting youth from inside the manor. But if we're right and the drug ring finds out what I am, they'll kill me as surely as they killed Greg."

"And if you succeed—" she drilled him with a pain-streaked glare "—you'll kill Hope Manor."

"That bothers you more, huh? Nice to know where I stand."

She jerked away from him. "That's not what I meant."

"Kids are dying, Kim. You have to see how it is. This drug ring must be stopped."

She stared out the window, hands clenched. Outside, the chain-link fence, silhouetted by storm clouds, looked downright menacing.

The minute he'd scaled that fence, he'd locked Kim into his plan as surely as the web of metal wires imprisoned these kids. "I know you want to believe the best of everyone, but someone here is not what they seem."

She spun around and dug her knuckles into her hips. "Yeah, I'm looking at him."

Ethan steeled himself against the barb. He had a job to do. He never should've let his emotions get involved. He positioned himself in front of the door, feet shoulder-width apart, arms crossed over his chest. "I need your promise that you won't give me up. We want the same things here."

"Oh, I don't think we do."

Kim slapped her pen down on the letter she'd been trying to draft and paced to the window of Dad's office. Holed up here since church let out, she'd managed to avoid running into Ethan, but the respite hadn't kept him from disrupting her every waking minute, not to mention the fitful scraps of sleep she'd snatched last night. She never should've let him talk her into giving him a twenty-four-hour reprieve.

Take some time to consider the consequences, he'd said. *Don't make a rash decision you might regret,* he'd said. *I never meant to hurt you,* he'd said.

Right!

He should've considered the consequences before he kissed her.

Tormenting herself, she revisited the moment. The tenderness of his hands cradling her face. The longing in his eyes. The sweetness of his kiss. With him, she'd felt as though she'd found a part of herself that she hadn't known was missing.

What an idiot. All he'd wanted was information.

She should blow his cover sky-high and see how *he* liked feeling betrayed.

Kids are dying.

Ethan's words reverberated through her mind once again.

"Oh, God, what am I supposed to do? I understand that Ethan has a job to do. That the job bound him to keep his true purpose here a secret. But did he have to make me fall for him to do that?"

She sank into Dad's chair and hugged her knees to her chest. She'd thought spending the afternoon in Dad's office would affirm yesterday's decision to fire Ethan, but peace eluded her. Her chest hadn't ached this badly since the day Dad confided that he had inoperable cancer.

And what if she did let him stay?

His investigation could destroy the manor. Didn't she have a loyalty to her father?

Why couldn't Ethan understand that?

The last thing I want to do is hurt you. What did he think destroying the manor would do to her?

But Ethan had said an investigation was inevitable, and a quiet one was better than one splashed across the newspapers. He was right, of course. If there was a drug dealer operating out of the manor, he had to be stopped. If only the investigation didn't jeopardize everything she held dear.

She jumped as a knock sounded behind her.

She braced her hand on the back of the desk chair and turned. "Come in."

Ethan slipped inside. From the dark smudges under his bloodshot eyes, he looked as though he'd gotten less sleep than her.

Had his claim that telling her about the investigation put his life at risk been more than a scare tactic?

He clicked the door closed behind him. "Have you made your decision?"

"I want you to know that I've prayed about this long and hard." She wavered. "The fact you're a cop—"

The door burst open, and Kim froze.

Darryl stepped inside, his gaze bobbing from her to Ethan.

Ethan shifted almost imperceptibly, blocking her from Darryl's view, giving her a moment to collect herself.

"What's up?" Darryl said, horning his way around him.

Ethan's gaze silently pleaded with her not to betray his confidence.

Right, like he deserved her cooperation after all his lies.

She blinked, startled by her abrupt resurgence of anger. She'd panicked at the sight of the door opening, afraid that whoever was there had overheard her call Ethan a cop. But they could trust Darryl. If he hadn't been out so late last night, she might've discussed her decision with him. She stepped around Ethan. "Ethan was telling me—"

Ethan coughed and lifted a book from the box on the chair. "I was telling Kim that she should give herself some time before making any *rash decisions* about what she does…with her dad's things."

Kim snatched the book from his hand. Telling Darryl the truth about Ethan was hardly rash. Unlike Ethan, she didn't keep secrets from those closest to her. Then again, the fewer people who knew why Ethan was here, the less likely his allegations would make headlines.

Kim fiddled with the corner of the book. Considering Darryl's dubious expression, she couldn't predict what his reaction to Ethan's secret might be. He clearly wasn't happy to find Ethan here with her. And Darryl hadn't exactly been on the same page as her when it came to protecting the manor's future.

She heaved a sigh. "Ethan's probably right. It's been so hard watching Dad's decline. I might be tempted to chuck something I'll regret." Like her good sense.

Darryl rested his hip on Dad's desk. "I'm surprised to see you in here on your day off. I thought you rescheduled your date with Aaron for after church." He snuck a glance at Ethan as if he expected him to be cheesed off.

"After church *tonight*. And it's a meeting, not a date."

"Right." The amusement in Darryl's eyes said she wasn't fooling anybody, which had to be more theatrics for Ethan's benefit, because if her little brother hadn't clued in yet that she wasn't interested in Aaron, he hadn't been paying attention.

"Was there anything else?"

Darryl stood. "Nope, I just stopped in to see why you were here." He gave Ethan a loaded nod. "I guess I'll see you later."

Ethan closed the door. "Thanks for not giving me up."

"I did it for the manor's sake. Not yours. Because, for the record, I intend to prove you wrong."

Ethan didn't so much as blink. "Starting with Aaron?"

"Maybe."

"Then you should know that I followed him to Harbor Park a couple of weeks ago. He met with a group of teens and one of them gave him a paper bag with packets of crack inside."

Kim tensed. No, Aaron wouldn't do drugs. "If the bag was paper, how'd you see what was inside?"

"I retrieved it from a Dumpster."

A laugh of relief burst out. "You're telling me he threw the bag away?"

"I know." Ethan pushed his fingers through his hair. "His behavior makes no sense."

Ethan's frustration was as palpable as the bite of her fingernails in her palms. Clearly, he wasn't making this stuff up. "It makes no sense," she said. "Unless…unless you were right about him trying to protect me. If he's been blackmailed into cooperating with this drug ring, he could be trying to mitigate the damage."

She shook her head. Now Ethan had her buying in to his crazy theories.

"I know you don't want to believe any of this, but I need you to keep an open mind. The sooner we figure this out, the sooner I'll be out of your life."

The pain in his eyes gave her an unwelcome jolt. Did she want him out of her life?

She pulled away. Of course she did. For all she knew, the look in his eyes was yet another calculated act designed to win her cooperation.

How was she going to deal with seeing him all the time?

She couldn't do this. She never should've agreed to keep his cover.

But what if he was right?

She couldn't bear to be responsible for the overdose of another teen. She'd just have to avoid Ethan. Yeah, avoid him. How hard could that be?

Apparently not as easy as she thought.

The next morning Kim sat behind the wheel of her car and stared up at Ethan's duplex. The sickly sweet smell of gumdrops permeated the air, evoking memories she'd been trying to forget. She wouldn't be here at all except that last night she'd done some digging of her own—into Aaron's past—and learned something Ethan needed to know if he didn't want to waste time investigating the wrong people.

"Kim?"

She jumped at the sound of a voice.

Ethan hunched to the level of her car window. "Sorry, I didn't mean to startle you. What are you doing here?" Perspiration slicked his corded skin and she realized he must've been out running.

"I, uh… We need to talk." She'd fill him in on what she'd learned about Aaron last night. *Then* she'd avoid him.

Ethan glanced at his watch. "Don't you start work in half an hour?"

"I called and told them I'd be late. I thought we could grab a coffee and go to the pier."

The smile toying with the corners of his mouth did funny things to her stomach. Maybe the pier wasn't such a good idea, considering what had happened the last time they'd parked by the lake. She cringed to think how easily she'd succumbed to his seduction.

"Give me a minute to wash up," he said. "Do you want to wait inside?"

Her gaze cut to the street and the tiny pinpricks that had

been needling the back of her neck stampeded down her spine. But admitting her fear would only fuel Ethan's theories.

She tightened her grip on the steering wheel. "I'll wait here. Thanks."

If she were honest with herself, something other than telling him about Aaron had propelled her here. She couldn't stop thinking about Ethan's edginess around Joy. She'd written off his reaction as concern that Joy might blow his cover.

But Joy hadn't known he was working undercover.

Sure, she'd assumed he was still a cop, but Kim had corrected her, as Ethan had to have known she would. And on other occasions when his identity might've been challenged—with Tony, with Darryl—Ethan hadn't acted the least bit ruffled.

He was hiding something more from her, and she needed to know what. She didn't want any more surprises.

TWELVE

Ethan and Kim carried their coffees to one of the benches along the pier. Squawking seagulls swooped around them in search of handouts. The water sparkled like a thousand diamonds in the early-morning light.

Ethan sipped his coffee, waiting for Kim to share what was on her mind. For her protection, he'd trailed her and Aaron last night, but he was sure she hadn't noticed. He'd hoped her conversation with Aaron would yield some insight into his role in the drug-running scheme. But after Kim's pledge to prove his theories wrong, Ethan hadn't expected her to rush over and divulge her findings.

He hadn't expected her to want to talk to him at all. He'd been a fool to think he could salvage their relationship by telling her the truth about his mission. She could never give her heart to the man destined to tear apart her father's life's work, even if she could forgive him.

After several minutes without a peep from Kim, Ethan said, "Did you and Aaron work out your presentation for the youth group?"

A sobering thought struck him. While he trusted Kim not to compromise his investigation deliberately, an inadvertent comment might've tipped Aaron off. Maybe he was the one who'd called the police station asking about him.

"We're going to tell the kids a few of the residents' stories.

Hopefully give them a picture of where they don't want to end up. And then we'll open the discussion for questions."

"And?"

Her head tilted, and the glint of sun on her hair revealed hints of red and gold he hadn't noticed before.

He resisted the urge to curl a wayward lock around his finger, even as he remembered the silky feel against his skin. He cleared the sudden clog in his throat. "You had something to tell me?"

"Yes, I asked Aaron if he knew of any teens that were using. He's suspicious of a few. Said he confronted them. No one admitted to anything, though, let alone snitched on suppliers."

"O-kay," Ethan said, curious why she felt compelled to skip work to tell him.

"But one girl told Aaron her boyfriend did drugs and was pressuring her to try them. A few days later, she called Aaron in a state because her boyfriend had hid his stash in her purse after he got stopped for speeding. Aaron convinced her to leave her boyfriend and then helped her dispose of the drugs."

"And you believe him?"

"The story explains what you saw."

"Maybe too well. Aaron is the interim director of a youth detention facility. If his story's true, he had a moral obligation to report the girl's boyfriend to the police and present the drugs as evidence."

Kim chewed on her bottom lip. "Okay, I see your point. But if he'd reported the incident, none of the kids would confide in him again."

"And because he didn't, her boyfriend could be Miller's Bay's next overdose victim."

Kim winced. "I never thought of it that way."

"Something to keep in mind when the board votes on whether to make Aaron's appointment permanent. I doubt they want a director prone to such serious lapses in judgment."

She frowned.

He let her stew on his remarks while he finished his coffee. "Was there anything else?"

"Yeah, one thing." Her expression changed. Her eyes lit with challenge. "About you."

His heart gave his ribs a hard kick. "Oh?"

"Yes. If you expect me to help you, you can't keep any more secrets from me."

"No problem, you figured out my one and only."

"I don't think so. You're hiding something else."

"How do you figure?"

"You don't strike me as the kind of person who'd be uneasy around someone simply because they're handicapped."

"I'm not."

"You are around Joy."

His throat thickened. He shifted his attention to the water, but its pristine beauty only made the ugly memories surface faster. She'd bull's-eyed his darkest secret. He crushed his coffee cup in his fist, tossed it into the trash and forced himself to face her. "Joy led me to the Lord. She's very dear to me. I can't imagine why you'd think otherwise."

"You went ashen at the mere mention of her name."

He buried his hands in his pockets, studied the ducks in the water. Okay, maybe a relationship with Kim wasn't in his future, but why give her another reason not to want him?

"Now you won't even look at me. You listen to me, Ethan. I'm in the middle of this investigation whether either one of us likes it or not. And Joy is around my family every day at the hospital. If she has something to do with this case, I need to know."

He pulled his hands from his pockets, splayed his fingers over his thighs, and let out a sigh. "She doesn't. Believe me."

Kim laid her hand on his arm. Her touch felt cool against his skin. Not unkind, but unrelenting. "When I told you I talked to Joy, you said she must've given me a thorough description of *the accident*. You meant Joy's accident, didn't you?"

"This has nothing to do with my case. Joy has nothing to do with my case," he growled, hating how callous he sounded. But he couldn't tell her what he'd done. Something inside him wouldn't let him feel even a whisper of hope that Kim could look at him without disgust if she knew the truth.

"I'm beginning to suspect that Joy has something to do with every one of your cases," Kim said softly.

Ethan gritted his teeth and gave his head a hard shake. "Let's just stick to this case. I've been down this road before. It's not pretty."

"I work with young offenders. Not pretty is my specialty."

Ethan tried to unlock his clenched muscles, to relax his shoulders, to sit back on the bench rather than on the edge with his hands gripped on his knees.

He'd almost succeeded until Kim coaxed him to meet her gaze. "I don't understand why thinking about Joy bothers you so much. She told me that you helped her through a tough time in her life."

"You're right. You don't understand." He lurched forward, but Kim caught his arm and forced him to stay seated.

"So explain it to me."

"Forget about it." His brusque response only made Kim tighten her hold.

"I can't do that, Ethan. As much as you hurt me with your deceptions, seeing you so tormented hurts me more."

Her unexpected mercy nearly undid him, and to his horror, he realized he was on the verge of tears. He fisted his hands, letting his nails chew into his palms to divert his thoughts. Bit by bit, the lump that had risen to his throat dissolved and the stinging in his eyes eased. How did the mere prospect of talking about something that had happened more than fifteen years ago have the power to derail him so completely?

Some undercover cop he'd turned out to be. He couldn't even keep his emotions under wraps.

"I know I have no right to probe into your private life,

Ethan. But I can see that whatever you're keeping bottled up is eating away at you. If you don't want to talk to me about it, you should talk to someone. Otherwise its hold over you will only grow stronger. The power of secrets is in keeping them secret."

Kim's invitation lay tantalizingly before him like a lifeline he longed to grasp. But he'd tried opening up once before. With Stephanie. And the only thing his confession had freed him from was her. "I don't deserve your sympathy. It's better you learn that now instead of later."

"Why don't you let me be the judge of that?"

Her voice was so soft, so sweet, her gaze so sincere, he felt as if a weight were being lifted from his shoulders. Maybe she was right. He certainly had nothing to lose. Not anymore.

He drew in a deep breath and stared out over the lake, letting his emotions go numb. "I'm the one who put Joy in that wheelchair."

He expected Kim to startle, gasp, wince, *something,* but she simply gave his arm a gentle squeeze. "Tell me how it happened."

Her calm acceptance cracked open the walls around his heart. And in that moment, more than anything, he wanted to trust her. He didn't care if his heart would be stripped in the process. She deserved the truth. He relaxed his clenched fists. Let the images tumble through his mind. "It was a beautiful day like this one. My buddies and I were heading to the beach to celebrate the end of school. Top down. Radio blaring. We were young, foolish and feeling invincible.

"The guys passed around a joint, and pestered me to try it. I took a short puff to get them off my back." He winced at how easily he'd given in. "The football team's quarterback and his car full of cronies picked that moment to pull alongside us on the two lane road. I let off the gas, but the car stuck to us like Velcro. 'Show him what you got,' the guys shouted, and I gunned the gas."

His gaze shifted to the shoreline, but in his mind's eye all he saw was the yellow line that marked the center of the road. "My car took the curve at double the speed limit. By the time I saw Joy…it was too late." He looked at her, but caught between the present and the past, his eyes couldn't focus. "One second Joy was running—strong, beautiful. The next she lay sprawled on the ground, her head wrenched at an impossible angle."

Kim smothered a gasp. "That's why you looked so panicked when you found me in the ditch." She cupped her hand over his. "You must've felt horrible."

"Still feel." He turned his palm up and felt as if he'd been granted a gift when Kim laced her fingers through his own. Realizing his mistake, he pulled away. "I don't deserve your pity. Now that you know what you wanted to hear, you should go."

She didn't move. "Joy has forgiven you, you know."

"I know."

"Don't you think it's time you forgave yourself? You can't change the past, but you can change what happens now."

Ethan bolted to his feet. "What do you think I've been doing for the past fifteen years? I lock up punks like me so women like you can feel safe jogging the streets."

Her face went white, and he mentally kicked himself for reminding her of the attacks against her yet again. Except… her gaze wasn't glazed as if she were reliving those incidents. It was fixed on something behind him.

He jerked his attention to the parking lot. "What is it?"

"The kid!" She squinted. "I think."

"The kid who vandalized your car and snatched your purse?"

A lone black SUV pulled onto the street and disappeared around the corner. Otherwise, the streets were empty. The shops not yet open. The water lapping the shoreline quickened to impatient slaps.

"Where? I don't see him."

"I'm not sure now. It was so far away." Kim's gaze remained fixed on the road. "I thought he climbed into that SUV."

"Did you catch the plate number?" Ethan yanked out his phone. "It's probably stolen."

"I don't think so." Her gaze shifted to his. "I recognized the driver. I think."

"Who?"

"The guy from the hospital. The one who stopped the kid from getting away."

What if Ethan tracked down the SUV?

Kim unlocked the admissions room door. She hadn't dared admit that she'd seen the driver exit her father's room a week ago. Ethan already thought her purse snatcher was connected to the drug ring as part of some convoluted blackmail scheme. His wild imagination would be connecting *Dad* to the drug ring next.

She dropped into the chair to wait for Melvin to return from court. The guy in the SUV was probably someone who helped street kids turn their lives around. Like Dad. It would explain why he'd visited Dad. If he was the same person.

But not why Dad had been so upset afterward.

She twisted the phone cord around her finger. Maybe she should've told Ethan. If he'd trusted her enough to admit to causing Joy's paralysis, how could she not trust him enough to admit her dad might know the man who'd picked up the kid?

What Ethan had shared was huge. No guy had ever opened up to her like that before. Nate would never have trusted her with that.

Of course, that's because Nate was untrustworthy.

Not that Ethan had been up-front with her about why he was really here. He'd wooed her to use her. Still...

If Dad knew the driver of the SUV, he could give them a name, tell them where they could find the person, so he could lead them to the kid. Of course, Ethan didn't need to know where she got the driver's name. She dialed Dad's hospital room.

Mom picked up the phone. "Kim? What's wrong?"

"Nothing. I just wanted to ask Dad something."

"He's sleeping at the moment. Had a bad night. He'll probably be out for a few hours. Anything I can help with?"

"Maybe. Dad had a visitor the night I wrecked my ankle. Do you know his name?"

Silence greeted her question.

"Mom? Did you hear me?"

"Yes…just trying to recall who it might've been. I'm not sure. Your father gets so many visitors. Why do you ask?" The cheery note in Mom's voice sounded more forced than usual.

Dad's illness was taking such a toll on her. Kim hated that Mom felt she had to put on a cheery front.

"Don't worry. It's not that important."

"I doubt your father would remember with all the pain meds he's on," Mom said, but Kim knew she meant *Don't upset him by asking him something he won't be able to remember.*

Kim ended the call. Now what?

She glanced at the clock. Melvin wasn't due back for a few more minutes. Should she call Ethan?

If Dad couldn't remember the name, what was the point?

In need of a little moral support, she called Ginny instead.

Ginny instantly guessed the reason for the call. "You talked to him, didn't you?"

"I had to know."

"Sometimes it's better to nix your compulsion to know what's bothering people. Especially when said person is a jerk."

"Ethan isn't a jerk." Clearly, telling Ginny about Ethan had been a mistake, but she'd needed to talk to someone after his cop revelation, and who safer than the wife of a cop?

"Kim, wake up. He's using you."

"Like Rick used you when you landed in the middle of *his* undercover investigation? Anyway, I was right. He did have another secret. But it has nothing to do with the manor."

"What is it?"

"Uh…I can't tell you. He shared the details in confidence."

"Don't let him suck you into a relationship. You're going to wind up hurt."

"This from the woman who's been harping on me to date more?"

"I was wrong."

"Well, you're in luck. I get the impression he doesn't think he's good enough for me."

"Or he's playing on your sympathies. I hate to tell you this, Kim, but you're a pushover for a sob story."

"Well, I'd rather be a pushover than callous." No matter why he was here and how he'd used her, she couldn't bring herself to look away from his pain. Guilt was eating him alive. There had to be some way to help him overcome his remorse for Joy's accident.

A police car pulled into the garage. "My arrival's here. I've gotta go."

"I know you want to help Ethan, but think about what I said. Okay?"

"Sure." But she could help him without getting her feelings involved. If she spent all her time worrying about not getting hurt, she'd never help anybody. Kim clicked off the phone and turned her attention to the officer holding Melvin.

While she signed the paperwork, the officer removed the youth's handcuffs.

Once free, Melvin ripped his hands from the officer's hold and rubbed at his chafed wrists. "Thanks for nothing."

The officer gave her one of those looks that said *He's your problem now,* and then left without a word.

Kim motioned Melvin toward the debriefing area where

prisoners were searched before returning to their unit. "How'd your hearing go?"

"How d'you think?" he said caustically.

"Not the way you hoped?"

He snorted. "Your brother can't fix squat."

"My brother?" How did he know she and Darryl were siblings?

They never used last names around the residents, or discussed relationships, for fear residents would use the information to manipulate them. If she'd been quicker, she would've asked, "What brother?" Instead, she said, "What's my brother got to do with your hearing?"

Melvin—the kid who got picked on by everyone, the kid who whimpered in his room at night when he thought nobody could hear, the kid she'd done her best to mentor over the past few months—glared at her with an icy sneer. "Like you don't know."

Refusing to rise to his bait, she waved toward the door. "Let's go."

"Or maybe you don't wanna know," he said over his shoulder.

She squared her jaw and escorted him in silence. Melvin wasn't the kind of kid who'd mess with people's minds. If not for Ethan's investigation, she would've assumed that Darryl offered to vouch for Melvin's good behavior, nothing more.

Instead, all kinds of troubling explanations preyed on her mind.

Not one of which she'd believe for a second.

"What a farce this place is," Melvin grumbled. "I'd have been better off at the detention center in Hamilton."

"Why do you think that?"

He stopped and faced her.

She imagined he was going for a fierce scowl, glaring down from his six foot three inches, but his reddened face atop his skinny frame looked like a sunburned scarecrow.

"You people talk about God and—" His gaze shifted abruptly. "You don't wanna know." He turned on his heel and stalked down the hall without another word.

Curious about what had caused Melvin to clam up, Kim glanced behind her.

Aaron stood outside his office door. He strode toward her. "Everything okay?"

"Sure." Right. The boy would be intimidated by the director's appearance, afraid of getting in trouble for mouthing off to staff. "Mel's just letting off steam."

"Glad to hear it," Aaron said. "Looking forward to the meeting tonight." He gave her a wink before heading back to his office.

Kim unlocked unit three's door and then, leaving Melvin in the common room, she stepped into the staff station to add his paperwork to his file. Aaron's appearance had reminded her of yet another matter she had to deal with—what to do about his lapse in judgment regarding the drugs the teen girl had given him. Aaron had shared the explanation in confidence, so Kim didn't feel right about relaying it to the board without discussing the matter with him. If he recognized the folly of his decision, as she had when Ethan had presented it to her, then perhaps nothing more needed to be done, except give the police a heads-up on the boyfriend.

She smiled, remembering the jealous undertone in Ethan's voice when he'd asked about her meeting with Aaron. Ethan had made it clear that he worried about her seeing Aaron because he was a suspect, but part of her liked to think there was more to Ethan's feelings than he wanted to admit.

She shook her head. The whimsical thought was nothing more than her mind's defense of her bruised ego. Her only interest in Ethan was to help him overcome the remorse that paralyzed him as completely as the accident that paralyzed Joy's legs.

And to keep him from destroying Hope Manor.

Distantly, she realized that someone was talking to her, but the words had been background noise to the clamor in her head.

Darryl stood at the door, a curious look on his face. "Did you hear anything I said?"

She forced her attention to him. "Sorry. My mind was somewhere else. But I'm glad you're here. Melvin's ticked with you. What's that about?"

"Beanpole? How should I know?" Darryl shot the kid a scowl through the staff station window. "You know how these kids operate. They're always pitting one staff member against another, making ridiculous accusations to divert attention from themselves."

"I hate it when you paint them all with the same brush. Just because one or two—"

"Never mind about that," Darryl said. "I asked where you were this morning."

Perplexed by the abrupt question, she said, "I had to see someone."

"Who?"

"None of your business."

"For crying out loud, Kim, it's not safe for you to go off before dawn without telling anyone where you're going."

"I called work, and Ginny knew. Lighten up."

"You don't understand how dangerous—"

"I understand you're my brother and you're worried about me, but we can have this discussion at home. We have work to do." Ever since the incident with Blake, Darryl had been checking up on her left, right and center. His smothering was driving her crazy.

Kim let herself back into the unit and couldn't help but notice how Melvin's gaze followed Darryl's movements. As much as she wanted to, she knew she couldn't ignore Mel's cryptic allegations. She plunked down beside the boy on the battered sofa.

"I know you don't think so, but I do want to know what's bothering you."

He shrugged.

"If a staff member has said or done something out of line, you can tell me."

"I never said nothin' like that."

"You said this place is a farce. That tells me you don't think we practice what we preach. Is that what you think?"

He shimmied to the far corner of the couch. "I was ticked 'cause the judge didn't give me probation."

"Is that the only reason?"

"I want to go to my room."

"Melvin, if something's bothering you—"

"I want to go to my room now."

"Okay, okay. But I want you to know that when you're ready to talk, I'm ready to listen."

His mouth said "Whatever." But his eyes said *You don't wanna know.*

She let him into his room. Clearly she had more to discuss with her brother than his overprotectiveness.

The changeover call sounded over the walkie-talkie.

Kim glanced at the clock through the staff station windows. At the sight of Ethan her heart jumped. He wasn't scheduled to work today. Why was he here?

He'd changed into jeans and a T-shirt, and he just stood there watching her. So she couldn't exactly pretend she hadn't seen him. Although…maybe he had some word on the kid.

She hurried to the staff station. The rest of the staff were with the residents, giving her and Ethan as much privacy as glass walls could afford. "You have news?"

An emotion she couldn't decipher shadowed Ethan's eyes. He averted his gaze. "I was called in for someone who's sick."

"Oh. So you didn't find…?"

"Sorry. No. Couldn't find the SUV. I asked the chief to have someone he trusts watch the alley. If the kid lives around there, they'll get him. Then you'll have to go to the station to ID him."

"But I have that youth meeting tonight."

"Not a problem. Could be a while before they catch him…" His voice trailed off, leaving *if they catch him* unsaid.

"Maybe some of the kids in the youth group can give us a lead."

"Yeah, I'd appreciate a full report." Ethan tipped his chin toward Mel's bedroom door. "What had Beanpole so nervous?"

Her gaze jerked to the window. Now that she thought about it, the boy had seemed nervous. "He had his hearing today."

"If the hearing's over, why's he still nervous?"

Recalling what Mel had said about Darryl, she shifted uncomfortably.

"Are you sure the hearing is all that's bothering him?" Ethan pressed.

"I have no idea." Well, she had some idea, but she wasn't about to voice it without talking to her brother first.

THIRTEEN

"Mom, do you know where Darryl is?" Kim asked, walking into the kitchen.

"Ouch." Her mom plopped a tray of cookies onto the stovetop and snatched back her hand, putting her thumb to her mouth. "Sorry, I didn't hear you drive in. How was the youth meeting?"

"Good." Except a summons to the police station had cut short her opportunity to glean information from the youths following the meeting. She shivered. The officer had said her purse-snatcher-slash-car-vandal couldn't see her through the one-way glass, but his soulless glare had chilled her to the core.

Mom glanced at the clock. "The meeting must've been good. Youth group never ended this late when you were a teen."

Kim helped herself to a cookie, pausing to savor the comforting aroma as she broke it in two and licked the melted chocolate. "I had a couple of errands to run. And I stopped to see Dad."

At least the vandal's arrest had spared her from having to ask Dad for help. She'd hoped to find Darryl there and have their conversation where Mom wouldn't overhear. Mom was already baking enough to feed a small army. She didn't need anything more to stress-bake over.

Like her son doing something shady.

"You were always the bright spot of your father's day." She motioned Kim to join her outside and settled heavily into a patio chair. "I don't know what's keeping your brother."

The garden lights spaced around the porch cast creepy shadows over the yard.

An image of the pockmarked teen pouncing from the darkness flickered through her thoughts, making her shiver yet again. She sank into a chair and let the familiar sounds of the night soothe her frayed nerves.

The chirrup of crickets. The warble of toads. The breeze whispering through the leaves.

Then the squeak of rusty hinges cut through the air.

Kim sprang to her feet and grabbed the first heavy object at hand.

The side gate slapped shut. "Hello? Kim?"

Ethan stepped into view, and Kim's breath escaped in a rush. "What are you doing sneaking around here?"

"That depends." He looked at the weapon in her hand and grinned. "You planning on braining me with Dopey?"

She looked down at the garden gnome she'd picked up. *Oh.* She let out a sheepish laugh. Then grinned back at him. "Well, if the gnome fits…"

He laughed, and Kim felt ridiculously pleased with herself. She set the lawn ornament back on its perch.

"I didn't mean to startle you. Nobody responded to my knocks, and I thought I heard voices back here." He nodded at Mom. "Hi, Mrs. Corbett."

Mom gave her a knowing look. "Nice to see you again, Ethan. Have a seat and I'll put on some tea." She scurried inside.

Great, her pathetic crush was obviously still alive and well and now Mom planned to feed it by plying Ethan with tea and home-baked cookies.

At least Ginny wasn't here to harp on Ethan's faults. And

Mom wouldn't be so hospitable, either, if she knew why Ethan was really hanging around her daughter.

Certain Ethan's impromptu visit had something to do with the kid's arrest, Kim tilted her head toward the open window above the kitchen sink and her eavesdropping mother, then led him to the back of the garden.

She stopped next to the old tire swing and fingered the heavy rope. "Please don't tell me the kid's already made bail," she whispered.

"No, his hearing won't be for a couple of days."

She let out a relieved sigh. "Did he give up the name of his partner—the one who slashed my tires?"

"He was pretty tight-lipped, the chief said. Except to say you needed to learn to mind your own business."

"Me? They're the ones who attacked my car for no reason."

"Oh, they had a reason—retaliation over your attempts to get Beanpole to quit their gang."

Shock streaked through her chest. "He said that?"

"More or less, yeah."

Kim sank onto the tire swing. "How would he even know? Only the residents' parents have phone and visitation privileges."

"Through another resident who'd been released, most likely. That kid who attacked you in the hall the other day is part of the same gang. They both have a sword tattoo at the base of their necks. I wouldn't put it past them to deliberately get arrested so they could get to you or Beanpole inside the manor."

The swing shook and she realized she was trembling.

Ethan steadied the rope. "The good news is that their attacks don't have anything to do with the drug ring. And now that the gang knows the police are on to them, you shouldn't have any more trouble."

"That's a relief." She could stop worrying about Ethan's silly blackmail theory. She'd gotten all worked up over Beanpole's "Darryl" comments for nothing.

"Just be on your guard."

The back door slapped open, and Darryl stalked down the steps toward them, his scowl obvious despite the deepening night. "Mom said you wanted to see me?"

Kim stiffened.

Ethan dropped his hand. "I'd better go," he said, and Kim felt a sense of relief. "You on tomorrow, Kim?"

"No."

"But you'll be at the basketball game tomorrow night, won't you?"

"Oh, yeah, I wouldn't miss it."

Ethan gave Darryl a curt nod and left by the side gate.

"What was he doing here?" Darryl demanded the second the gate squeaked shut.

"Visiting. And I'd appreciate it if you stopped acting like a belligerent ogre around my friends. You're carrying your protective-brother routine too far. Every guy who talks to me is not another Nate. Got it?" She jolted at her own words—well, Ginny's words, more like.

Wouldn't Ginny be thrilled that her advice was finally sinking in—about Ethan?

Darryl grabbed the tire swing, and halted her frenetic movements. "Who did you meet this morning? It was Ethan, wasn't it?"

"What if it was?"

"We don't know him from Adam. You go off without telling us where you're going or with whom, and then you don't show up for work. What am I supposed to think?"

"What did you think?" she said, shocked by his implication.

He scraped his palm down his face. "I thought...horrible things, Kim."

Her heart clenched. Worry lines creased his forehead, and shadows blackened the skin beneath his eyes. Although younger than her by three years, he looked years older. She understood all too well how Dad's illness and the future preyed on the mind. Yet the responsibility he felt for their family weighed on him more than she'd realized. "I'm sorry. It never occurred to me that you'd be so worried."

"You're too trusting."

"You make that sound like a bad thing."

"It is. Not everyone is as kind-hearted as you. You…" He hesitated. Then shook his head.

"I what?"

He exhaled. "You need to be careful."

"I met with Ethan to discuss strategies for saving the manor. Nothing more."

"Your welfare is more important than your crusade," Darryl exploded. "I don't understand you. You act as if saving the manor is going to keep Dad alive. But it won't. You should be spending as much time as you can with him, because once he's gone, none of it will matter anymore."

She felt as though she'd been punched. She stared at her brother in shock.

"Darryl," Mom scolded from the kitchen window, "that's enough."

Darryl stalked into the house. Kim could hear him stomp up the stairs and slam his bedroom door.

Kim hugged her knees and buried her face. *Saving the manor mattered. It had to matter.* Deep down she knew Darryl's outburst was nothing more than grief lashing out, but his accusations still hurt.

The screen door creaked open, sprang closed again. Soft footfalls moved toward her.

"Your brother didn't mean that the way it sounded." Mom tucked a loose strand of hair behind Kim's ear the way she used to when Kim was a girl. "I've asked too much of him these past few months, more than either of us could've foreseen." She held her palm against Kim's cheek. "When your father dies—"

Kim cringed. Okay, they all knew the situation was bad, that eventually Dad was going to...

But they weren't supposed to *say* it! What was wrong with her family?

"Honey," Mom said gently, squeezing her hand. "When the time comes, Darryl will need your support more than ever."

"Am I wrong to want to save the manor?"

"No, honey. Your father is a good man. Seeing his work come to nothing would break his heart." Mom's gaze drifted to Darryl's bedroom window. "In our own way, that's what each of us is trying to make sure doesn't happen."

Ethan surveyed the spectators packing the benches along the gym wall. Extra staff had been brought in to keep an eye on the residents during their game against the visiting Bay Community Church Youth Group. Kim sat front and center manning the scoreboard. Her hair, caught up in a ponytail, drew attention to her high cheekbones and sparkling green eyes.

And why was he torturing himself noticing things like that?

He'd have to talk to her after the game, find out if she'd learned anything from last night's youth meeting. He'd intended to do that last night, but Darryl's interruption had nixed the opportunity.

He expelled a breath. With the revelation that the attacks on Kim—except maybe Blake's—had no connection to his investigation, he was getting nowhere fast on this case.

Shouts from the spectators drew his attention back to the game.

A Bay Community player slapped the ball out of Curt's hand, broke away and scored.

Kim added another two points to Bay Community's side of the scoreboard, and then threw Ethan a discouraged look.

He called for a time-out. "Okay, guys, we're down six points. If we want to close that gap, we've got to play as a team."

"Yeah," the team chorused.

"Beanpole was wide open under the net the last time you got the ball, Curt. Keep your eyes open."

Curt's lip curled and he grunted a noncommittal response. He'd been in a foul mood for two days, but this time, nothing Ethan tried had coaxed the kid into telling him what was bothering him.

Ethan clapped his hands. "Okay, team, let's show them what we've got."

The guys jogged back onto the court to the whoops and cheers of the staff and other residents. The ref tossed the ball between Beanpole and a Bay player, who had to be half a foot shorter. Beanpole knocked the ball to Curt, who passed it to Craig, who dribbled it up to the net and at the last second passed it around his back to Beanpole.

Beanpole slam-dunked the ball, and the crowd went ballistic.

"That's the way," Ethan yelled, clapping his hands. "Good job."

Kim added two points to their side of the scoreboard and beamed at him.

He winked, pleased that, if nothing else, at least they could share their delight in their unit's teamwork.

In short order, his boys scored four more points, bringing the crowd to their feet as the clock ticked down.

Curt stole the ball from the opposition and dribbled down the court. The church kids double-teamed him, blocking every attempt to drive his way to the net.

Ethan cupped his hands around his mouth and yelled, "Pass the ball."

The opposition wouldn't let Curt pass the ball forward, so Beanpole ran from under the net to half court. Curt bounce-passed the ball to him, drilled through the guys blocking his way, and turned just in time to tip Beanpole's lob over the lip of the net.

The crowd exploded. The Hope Manor team high-fived their way around the room, while Bay's team engaged in some good-natured ribbing.

After the teams shook hands, Bay Community's youth pastor—an engaging combination of linebacker and fun-loving mascot—invited everyone to gather around.

The residents sat cross-legged on the floor in front of him. They knew he'd once been in their shoes and gave him their full attention.

"You have dwelt long enough on this mountain," he said forcefully.

"This ain't no mountain," Tyrone answered back, and the other residents laughed.

"Don't be so sure," Pastor John responded with a good-humored lilt. "How many of you have heard the story of Moses leading the Israelites out of Egypt to the Promised Land?"

Three-quarters of the group raised their hands.

"Did you know they ended up wandering in the wilderness for forty years? Forty years! No wonder God told the Israelites they'd wandered around long enough. The Bible says the direct route was only an eleven-day journey. Can you believe that? Forty years to get somewhere that should've taken eleven days."

"What a bunch of idiots," one of the teens commented.

Ethan shot a glance at Kim. She'd hunkered down on the floor between a couple of residents. She must've sensed him watching her because she looked his way with a serene smile.

"Ah, you might not want to be too quick to judge them," Pastor John went on, making eye contact with one teen after another. "When I read this story in my Bible the other day, it occurred to me that most of us do exactly the same thing the Israelites did. We keep going around and around the same mountain."

An uncomfortable twinge fingered the pit of Ethan's stomach.

"We spend years wallowing in our circumstances, making

excuses about why we can't overcome them, instead of drawing on God's power to fight our way out of the wilderness and reach for the Promised Land." Pastor John's gaze fell on Ethan.

A sour taste welled in his throat. He slid his gaze in Kim's direction.

Her head tilted and she lifted an eyebrow.

If he didn't know better, he'd think she set him up.

"But there's some things ain't no way we can overcome," Beanpole argued, and Ethan silently cheered him on.

"That's what the Israelite spies thought about the giants living in the Promised Land—the giants they had to fight if they wanted to claim their inheritance. God had performed all kinds of miracles in Egypt. He parted the Red Sea. He fed them manna from heaven. But even after all that, the Israelites didn't believe God was bigger than those giants.

"So they wandered in the wilderness. If that's where you're at tonight, my question to you is, how big is your God?"

Ethan eyed the exit. The group squirmed.

Mercifully, Pastor John cut his sermon short with a clap. "It looks like the snacks have arrived. You've been a great group. Thanks for having us." He pointed to the back wall. "What do you say we eat?"

Shouts of agreement went up and the staff steered the residents in a semiorderly fashion past the table of baked goods Mrs. Corbett had generously provided.

Ethan hung back. His revelations to Kim had dug up too many regrets and thrown him off his game. He needed to regroup and focus on the job.

Kim stepped beside him, shoulder to shoulder, her gaze on the residents they were there to supervise. "Powerful message."

"I believe in God," he said, knowing exactly what she was up to, although he couldn't believe she'd still bother with him after everything he'd told her.

"I know you do, Ethan. But you're living in the wilderness."

"Yeah, well, you know what they say. It's a jungle out

there." He crossed his arms over the fresh ache starting to build in his chest.

The pastor walked over to them, and Kim thanked him for coming. As the man moved on, greeting others, Kim shifted her gaze back to the residents around the dessert table. "Why can't you see that by clinging to your remorse, you're strangling the joy God wants you to have?"

"I really don't want to have this conversation."

To the rest of the room, they might've appeared as though they were discussing the residents, which made the relative privacy a perfect opportunity to find out if she'd learned anything helpful last night. "I didn't get the chance to ask you last night how your talk with the youth group went."

"Remember what you said about Curt?"

"Which time?" Ethan asked, relieved that she'd dropped the other subject so easily.

"You told him that unless he saw the truth about the situation with his parents, instead of his guilt-skewed version of what happened, he'd never move on."

Irritation burned in Ethan's chest. "You're talking about me?"

She shrugged. "Just thinking out loud."

"I was street racing while smoking a joint," Ethan hissed through gritted teeth. "There's nothing guilt-skewed about it."

He welcomed the rush of anger, concentrating on it to get through the remorse that rushed in behind it. He turned to Kim. "What part of *I don't want to have this conversation* didn't you understand? You want to psychoanalyze somebody, try a resident. I have work to do."

FOURTEEN

Kim escorted the church group to their van, then wavered, uncertain whether she should hang around until the end of Ethan's shift. She hated to leave things the way they were. She'd wanted to help him, not alienate him.

Then again, maybe she needed to give Pastor John's message time to work on his heart.

Yeah, that was probably the way to go. Kim pulled out her keys and headed for her car at the far end of the parking lot. The starless night immediately draped her in darkness. She looked up and saw that two of the light standards had blown bulbs. *Strange.*

She quickened her pace, making a mental note to notify maintenance in the morning.

In the distance coyotes yipped.

She clicked her remote to unlock the car door, and automatically scanned the interior before slipping inside.

The coyotes' frenzied yips grew closer. A rabbit screeched, then silence.

Kim yanked the door closed and hit the lock. The coyotes that roamed the fields and woodlands surrounding the detention center posed little danger, but that didn't stop her stomach from tightening at the thought of the poor rabbit's fate.

Shaking the image from her mind, Kim started the car and pulled forward.

Thunk!

She braked, but as she shifted into Park so she could step out and take a look, a shadow crossed her rearview mirror.

Her heart jumped. She rammed the car back into Drive and floored the gas pedal.

The steering wheel fought her hold, but she managed to work the car to a noisy stop near the staff entrance. There, spotlights on the building pushed back the blackness.

Twisting in her seat, she squinted into the bushes near where she'd been parked.

Everything was still.

She let out a self-deprecating snort. What was she afraid of? The kid who'd been targeting her was behind bars. And with the cops on to his gang, none of his buddies were likely to try anything. At least, that's what Ethan had said—if not that convincingly.

She climbed out of the car. Her rear tire on the passenger side was flat.

The tension in her stomach eased. *Just a flat.*

Ethan had her so keyed up, she was seeing bogeymen everywhere. She popped her trunk and grabbed the lug wrench and jack. She fitted the wrench onto the first lug nut and heaved, but the nut wouldn't budge. She stood and bore all her weight onto it. Nothing.

She could call the auto club, but…asking Ethan to help her would be a perfect excuse to talk to him again, tonight. She glanced at her watch. Nine-thirty.

All but a few of the honor-level residents would be locked in their bedrooms by now. Ethan would be off in another half hour or so. She locked the car and headed back inside.

By the time she reached unit three, Curt was the only resident still up. He and Ethan sat on the couch in the common area chitchatting. If not for the locked doors and bars on the windows, they'd look like two friends shooting the breeze.

Not wanting to interrupt, Kim took a seat in the staff station to catch up on paperwork. Every once in a while, she glanced at the pair, but because the TV was on she couldn't hear what they said, although the conversation seemed to be getting pretty intense.

"What's *she* doing here?" Curt's voice boomed over the drone of the TV.

Kim looked up at the same time that Ethan swung his attention to the staff station. His eyes met hers and his surprise morphed into a scowl.

"Oh, man, I ain't tellin' you nothin'," Curt said. "Nothin'."

Kim tensed. What was that about?

Leon, the college student scheduled to work through the night in the unit, came out of the laundry room, where he'd probably been pulling a resident's laundry from the dryer.

Ethan said something to him, and Leon escorted the boy to his locker.

Eyes blazing, Ethan stormed into the staff station. "What are you doing here?"

Kim's jaw dropped, and her explanation detoured on the way from her brain to her mouth. She hitched her thumb in the direction of the door. "I... My tire's flat. I thought..." She picked up her purse. "Never mind. I'll call the auto club."

Ethan's shoulders sagged, and the fire in his eyes snuffed out. "No, I'm sorry. I can change your tire. It's just that Curt had been on the verge of spilling a name. I'm sure of it. And when he saw you, I guess he got scared."

"A name? You mean the inside guy?"

"Yeah, I was hoping. He said someone had offered him a job when he gets out."

Dread balled in Kim's throat. She hadn't wanted to believe Ethan's theory, but if it was true, the sooner the person was routed the better. She forced an encouraging tone to her voice. "I'm sure you'll be able to win Curt over again. You're really good with these kids."

Ethan shifted, looking uncomfortable with the praise. "I know what they're feeling."

"And that's not a bad thing, Ethan."

His eyes filled with a longing so raw she had to drop her gaze, focus on his bristly cheek, the tiny cleft in his chin. She wished with all her heart that there was some way she could help him break free of the remorse that imprisoned him. "God can use your troubles for good, if you let him."

"Don't start." Ethan turned away, busied himself with paperwork.

But she couldn't stop herself. "Joy helps countless people face heartbreaking situations because she's used her troubles to let God speak through her."

Ethan's pen stilled, but he didn't look up. "She's a remarkable woman."

"No more remarkable than you. You identify with these boys in a way most of us can't. And you were Joy's inspiration. She told me that helping you gave her purpose."

"Kim, I really don't want to talk about this."

"Joy showed me the card you sent her when you graduated from the police academy. Getting that card turned her life around. Did you know that she still carries the card in her purse?"

Ethan's gaze lifted. "I didn't know that." He looked away, but not before Kim saw the sheen of moisture in his eyes.

Kim's heart pounded. Everything in her felt certain that if he were forced to confront his guilty feelings, he could overcome them. She drew in a deep breath and plunged ahead. "The difference between you and Joy is that she brings a heart full of love and joy to everything she does, while you bring your whole heart with sadness and guilt."

Ethan's shoulders tensed, but he didn't meet her eyes. He turned back to the day's log.

Kim stifled a sigh of disappointment as Leon entered the staff station.

"Kim has a tire that needs changing," Ethan said expressionlessly. "So I thought we'd do the room checks a few minutes early."

"No problem."

The two men left the staff station, and Kim sank into a chair. Her insides quivered from her daring to confront Ethan like that. She prayed the attempt would make a difference.

Her thoughts revisited what he'd said about Curt and how peculiar it was that Curt had suddenly gotten defensive. She flipped through the logbook to see which staff had been on this unit in the past couple of weeks. Perhaps she could figure out who else had a tête-à-tête with Curt. The easiest time to chat privately with a resident was after everyone was confined to their rooms for the night. But like tonight, Leon had been on all week. Surely Curt wouldn't have been about to snitch on Leon when he was standing in the next room.

Kim scanned the daily records again. Curt had been to the computer lab and the weight room—both fairly private locations, and privileges that should've been revoked after he'd socked Melvin. And in both instances, the guard who'd escorted Curt was...

Darryl.

Ethan appeared and Kim slapped the book closed. If he noticed the way her heart pounded out of her chest, he didn't comment. "All set?"

Not trusting her voice, she nodded and scrunched her purse in her hands to hide the way they shook. Could it really be Darryl?

No way. Not her own brother.

But if she suspected him, even for a second, for sure Ethan would suspect him. She needed to prove Darryl's innocence. Search his room. Check the phone records on his cell. Confront him.

In the hallway, Ethan said, "You never did tell me about last night's youth meeting."

Relieved that he didn't ask her about the log, she plunged into a detailed account of the evening. Belatedly, she realized that he'd probably wanted to avoid a repeat of their earlier conversation. She told him about her talk with Dina Moyer, a foster child the youth pastor worried was using, and the way Dina had clammed up when Aaron joined them. "But since I brought Aaron to the meeting, I don't think she would've talked to me at all if she was afraid of him. Her reaction just struck me as unusual because most of the teen girls fawn over him, and because Mel had a similar reaction to him earlier that same afternoon."

"When he was acting so nervous?"

"Yeah."

"Tell me exactly what Beanpole said to you."

Kim hesitated. She didn't want to mention her brother's name.

Ethan returned his manor keys to the lockbox and retrieved his belongings from his locker. "Kim?"

"I can't remember, exactly. He was upset because he didn't get parole. He said this place is a farce, and I assumed he meant that we don't practice what we preach. I challenged him on that because I wanted to figure out where his hostility stemmed from. He said I didn't want to know. He told me that a couple of times."

Ethan stopped in the middle of punching the exit code in the door. "Why? What do you think he was talking about?"

"I have no idea."

"Did he mention any names?"

Kim replayed Melvin's words in her mind. *Your brother can't fix squat. Your brother.* "No, no names."

Ethan scrutinized her.

Uncomfortable with the intensity of his gaze, she punched in the remaining code and pushed through the door.

To her relief, he dropped the subject and followed. "I'll grab a tin of WD-40 from my trunk to spray on your tire bolts."

While he went to his car, Kim once again pulled the jack and lug wrench from her trunk. "Lord, please, don't let Darryl be involved in anything bad."

"Pardon?"

Ethan's deep voice made Kim jump.

"Sorry, I didn't mean to frighten you. I thought you were talking to me."

"Just thinking aloud." She handed him the wrench and set the jack on the ground.

Ethan reached inside the trunk and freed the spare from its crypt beneath the mat. "You'll have to get your tire fixed tomorrow because this one's just a donut." He squatted next to the flat and ran his hand over the rubber. "Were you parked here all night?"

"No, I was parked at the far end, but I couldn't see to change the tire there."

Ethan's gaze shifted past her and skimmed the darkness. "Why don't you come around to this side of the car and I'll show you how to loosen a rusty lug."

The last thing she wanted was a mechanic's lesson. She needed to get home before Darryl so she could search his room. But Ethan seemed to be waiting for her, so she squatted beside him and dutifully listened to his explanation.

After he changed the tire, he checked the brake lines and under the hood before giving her the green light to climb in. "I'll follow you home."

"That's okay, thanks. I'm sure I won't have any more trouble."

Unless she counted the trouble waiting for her at home.

Ethan stared after Kim's car. He knew he shouldn't have offered to follow her home, but he hadn't been able to stop the words from jumping out of his mouth. He'd been too preoccupied with the notion that someone might've let the air out of her tire...deliberately.

He chalked the impulse up to paranoia. Although it occurred to him that she might've let out the air herself to furnish an excuse to harangue him some more, he really didn't think she was cunning enough to have thought of that. But she'd certainly taken advantage of the opportunity.

Ethan shook his head. He never should've snapped at her the way he did. No wonder she couldn't get away from him fast enough. And as much as he deserved her rebuff, it still hurt.

Ethan mulled over their conversation. She meant well. And, okay, maybe she had a point. A lot of times he did feel as if he were wandering around in the wilderness like the youth pastor said. But saying he forgave himself wasn't going to make Joy walk again. No matter how contented Joy pretended to be, deep down Ethan knew he'd stolen her dreams of having a husband and children.

And if Joy couldn't have those things, *he* certainly didn't deserve them.

The night swallowed Kim's taillights and Ethan felt himself sinking, descending to that cold, black place where regrets shrouded every ray of sunlight God sent his way. Where guilt ate at him like cancer, poisoning all his relationships.

When Joy had offered him forgiveness all those years ago he'd felt utterly unworthy. He'd thought the way to deserve her gift was to become a cop. He remembered his youthful logic. He thought that if he could make the world a safer place, then at least some good would come out of his mistakes. But the next arrest and the next and the next were never enough. The only satisfaction in his career was the grim certainty that he'd served another day of penance.

He considered Kim's point that maybe the answer wasn't in atoning for his actions, but in learning to accept the way things were, learning to be grateful for Joy's forgiveness, learning to pass it on to others.

Lord, You know I believe in You. Working with these kids, seeing how lost they are, remembering how lost I once felt, has made me want to share Your love with them. I want them to see that You can change lives, renew people's hearts. But if Kim's right, if all people see is my remorse, how can I help them?

Curt came to Ethan's mind. Initially, Ethan feared that the rapport he'd established with the boy would scare off their suspect. But Curt's recent uneasiness had convinced Ethan that contact had been made. Ethan needed a name, but he also wanted to ensure Curt didn't get sucked in. So, what had gone wrong?

Why had Curt suddenly thrown up all the walls Ethan had painstakingly torn down?

You don't want to know.

Beanpole's words to Kim jolted Ethan's thoughts. She'd seemed nervous when recounting their discussion…as if she was afraid he would read too much into it. But he already knew someone in this operation was dirty. She was the one who didn't want to know.

Ethan hurried to the staff entrance. Apparently, he'd been talking to the wrong resident.

"What are you doing in my room?" Darryl growled.

Kim started at his sudden appearance, and then quickly shoved closed the drawer she'd been searching. She hadn't found anything to connect him to any wrongdoing at the manor.

A scrap of paper fluttered to the carpet. She picked it up and gasped at the name scrawled above a phone number. *Greg.* Kim sank onto the edge of the bed.

Darryl snatched the paper from her hand and crumpled it in his fist. "It's nothing."

"Don't you dare tell me it's nothing. Greg's dead. What do you know about that?"

The stricken look on Darryl's face cut off her breath. He stalked down the stairs.

"Don't you dare walk out on me," she shrieked, chasing after him. "We need to talk."

He detoured into the living room, picked up the remote control and flicked off the TV. By the time he dropped into a chair, he looked so utterly defeated Kim's heart wrenched.

He inhaled as if it took all his energy to draw a breath. "I don't know what to do anymore."

Her stomach knotted. "Do about what?"

Mom appeared in the doorway, a dusting of flour in her hair and oven mitts on her hands. She and Darryl exchanged a loaded glance. The kind of glance Kim had only ever seen twice before—the first time she'd been assigned to a suicide watch, and the night Dad had told her he had cancer. When Kim asked Dad about his prognosis, he'd given Mom that look and then said, "Excellent." Six months later he was admitted to the hospital. In the case of the suicide watch, the youth had claimed he was fine, but the nurse's eyes said "Don't believe him." Six hours later, he was dead—strangled himself with a bedsheet.

Mom perched on the sofa beside Kim and, with a calm deliberateness, removed one oven mitt at a time. "Darryl's just upset about your car trouble. I assured him it was nothing."

Kim's gaze ping-ponged between Mom and Darryl. "No, that's not it. Is it, Darryl? You don't know what to do about what? Greg? Me? The manor? What?"

With each question, Darryl's cheek muscles flinched. He raked his fingers through his hair. "Yes."

The knot in Kim's stomach tightened. *He's my brother, Lord. Please don't let it be my brother.* "Yes to which one?"

"All of them." His voice sounded beyond tired. Beaten.

Kim swallowed hard. "About the drugs, too?"

The remorse in Darryl's eyes tore at her soul.

"Why?" she breathed, drawing in barely enough air to be audible.

"It's my fault," Mom said. "For your father's sake, I begged him to do what Derk asked."

"Who's Derk?"

Darryl exhaled. "I think he might be the head of the drug ring that's moved into Miller's Bay."

The drug ring? Mom had begged him to listen to the head of a drug ring? This couldn't be happening. "Why on earth would you do what a drug lord tells you?"

Darryl and Mom exchanged another look.

A sense of foreboding gripped Kim's heart. "And what does any of this have to do with Dad?"

"Derk said he could prove Dad was an accessory—" Darryl broke off and swallowed.

"An accessory to *what?*"

"Murder."

FIFTEEN

Murder? No way.

Kim stared across the living room at her brother in disbelief. "And you believed him?"

"No. Not at first. Not until I talked to Mom."

"What?" Her gaze swung to Mom, who gave her a sad smile.

Kim dug her fingers into the edge of the sofa cushion, feeling as if the floor had opened into a gaping hole and everything she held dear teetered at the precipice.

"Derk told me that if I didn't do what he said, he'd ruin Dad." Darryl's words barely registered as Kim grappled to absorb the shock. "Ruin everything he'd worked for. Ruin his family."

"When your father was young," Mom explained, and Kim tried to focus, "he got caught up with this Derk fellow. They planned a robbery together, but it went bad. Derk shot the guard."

"Dad's a *felon?*"

Kim's heart jammed in her throat. Dad was the most honest, God-fearing man she knew. How could he have this dark past he'd never told her about?

"Your dad never got caught. He ran and didn't stop running for days. He ended up in Miller's Bay, tired, hungry and penniless. A farmer took him in and gave him a job. Remorse ate at him. The family took him to church, and your father drank in the message of forgiveness. He soon gave his life to the Lord and felt called to start a ministry for troubled boys. Eventually, that ministry became Hope Manor."

The room swayed. *Dad had been one of those boys.* She gripped the sofa arm. "Derk killed the guard?"

"Yes, but your father didn't know the man had died. Soon after I got pregnant with you, he read about Derk's murder trial in the newspaper. Your father wanted to go to the police immediately and turn himself in, but I begged him not to. He'd turned his life around, was doing good work. We were having a baby. I couldn't believe God would want him to sacrifice it all out of some misguided sense of doing the right thing."

Mom enfolded Kim's hand in hers. "I know my selfishness kept Dad from doing what he felt he needed to do to make things right. He tried to hide it, but I could see how he wrestled with bouts of guilt."

Just like Ethan. Guilt had to be Satan's most powerful weapon to keep believers from experiencing the fullness of God's love. "What does this Derk guy expect to prove?"

"I don't know. But if he exposes your father's past, innuendos will color people's perceptions of everything he's worked for."

The explanation skittered across Kim's mind like the spray of gravel from Blake's tires. And her heart pinched in acknowledgement. "Everyone in town will jump on the 'close Hope Manor' bandwagon." No matter what she did, Hope Manor and the kids they tried to help would become the ultimate casualties.

"I couldn't bear to let your father see that happen," Mom went on. "Not when he'd wanted to do the right thing all along. I was the one who didn't trust God enough to take care of us."

Darryl squeezed Mom's shoulder. "Since Dad wasn't expected to live more than a few weeks, Mom asked me to go along with Derk's demands. It didn't seem like that big a deal.

We'd planned to explain everything to the police as soon as Dad died."

"But your father has been hanging on for months," Mom added, "and Derk's demands persisted."

"This is crazy. Dad wouldn't want you to do something illegal to protect him. We should go to the police, now."

"No," Mom snapped. "I don't want your father tormented by that man. Your father deserves to die in peace."

"Yes. But kids are *dying* from these drugs. Do you want that on your conscience?"

"Kids who want to use drugs will get them whether Darryl steers them to Derk or not."

"Mom, get your head out of the oven! We're not talking about kids just getting high."

Mom's eyes sparked, but Kim was too furious to apologize.

"Three kids have died of overdoses," she hissed. "All of them former residents. Residents Darryl recruited."

"What?" Mom's startled gaze jerked to Darryl. "What's she talking about? You never told me anyone died."

Darryl's expression twisted. "More than Dad's reputation is at stake."

"Yeah," Kim said, her tone caustic enough to eat through his excuses. "You broke the law. You knew there'd be consequences."

"I'm not talking about me. I don't care about me. They can throw me in jail and throw away the key for all I care. I never should've let Mom talk me into this crazy plan. But this guy has people everywhere. Powerful people. *That's* how those kids ended up dead."

Mom wrung the oven mitts in her hands, looking horrified. "I didn't know. I never should've asked you to go along with him."

"You didn't know what kind of work Derk was offering the kids I recruited for him." Darryl's voice hitched. "I had assumed petty theft, the kind of stuff expunged from the records of young offenders once they hit eighteen. Then after Jake got picked up for selling drugs and wound up dead in the holding cell, I realized I couldn't go to the police because Derk must have someone on the inside. I knew I had to get evidence of what he was doing.

"I asked Greg to pretend to cooperate with him and report back to me. Only, Derk must've figured out that Greg intended to double-cross him."

"And you let him die!" Kim cried out. "You knew what Derk was capable of."

"What was I supposed to do?"

"You could've talked to Rick. You know he's not a dirty cop. We'll call him right now." Kim reached for the phone.

Darryl grabbed her hand. "We can't."

"Yes, we *can*." She yanked her hand free and started dialing. "You can't let kids die to protect Dad."

Darryl slapped his finger over the disconnect button. "This isn't about Dad anymore."

She pried off his finger. "No, it's not. Because doing what's right is more important here."

A car—Ethan's Impala—barreled into the driveway.

Kim rushed to the front door. It was past midnight. What was Ethan doing here? Did he already know about Darryl?

Darryl plowed his hands through his hair and paced the room, wild-eyed. "You've got to trust me. I'm going to do the right thing. I don't intend to let another person die."

Ethan stepped out of his car and rested his arm atop the door. The interior light spilled in a puddle on the ground. "Come on," he called to her over the car's roof. "That foster kid from church is missing. And I think I know where to find her."

Kim grabbed her purse and ran to the car. "How'd you hear Dina was missing?"

"Her foster mother called the police."

Ethan shoved open the passenger door from the inside, and

Kim climbed in automatically, as if they always went off chasing teenage runaways together. "Where do you think she is?"

"A stretch of beach down the shore from Harbor Park." In one move, he shifted into gear and roared out of the driveway. "I found a bunch of teens partying there the other night. All of them stoned." His hands twisted on the steering wheel. "I told the chief to send regular patrols. I should've followed up, made sure they happened."

"She might've snuck out to meet a boy. Maybe lost track of time."

"Does she have a boyfriend?"

The lights of the town shrank behind them, leaving only his headlights to cut through the yawning darkness ahead.

"I don't know. She was alone at the youth group meeting." Deep down, Kim knew that the only reason she'd made the suggestion was because she didn't want her brother blamed for another tragedy. She swallowed, searching for the right words to tell Ethan.

The car rattled down a rutted, grassy lane leading to a secluded stretch of beach. No cars or kids were in sight.

"The cops must've already cleared the place out." Ethan sounded worried. As if maybe the wrong cops had done the clearing. He stopped abruptly, handed her a flashlight and jumped out. "Come on. This way."

The distinctive smell of marijuana smoke hit her nostrils the instant she climbed from the car. She hoped that was the worst Dina had done. "Dina," Kim shouted. "Dina, are you here?"

The scream of a killdeer pierced the darkness and, feigning a broken wing, the bird tried to lure them away from its haphazardly constructed nest.

"Dina," she called, cupping her hands around her mouth.

A mess of footprints covered the ground around the remnants of a bonfire. Ethan held his hand to it. "Still warm."

"Dina! It's Kim Corbett. I want to help you."

At the edge of the dunes a bush rustled.

"This way." Ethan darted up the dune.

Kim scrambled after him. Damp sand seeped into her shoes and the chilly breeze cut through her shirt. The temperature dipped so low near the lake at night, Dina could be suffering from drugs *and* exposure.

Ethan flung aside branches. "She's not here."

"Dina," Kim shouted again.

A weak noise sounded to their left.

Kim's flashlight caught a reflective strip of cloth among the leaves. "Over there." She pointed.

Ethan reached Dina first. He fell to his knees and immediately checked her breathing. "She's alive."

Thank You, Lord. Kim steadied her trembling hand on Ethan's shoulder.

In the dim beam of their flashlights, Dina's eyes looked vacant.

"We've got to get her to a hospital," Ethan said, lifting her in his arms. "Call her parents and let them know we're bringing her in."

Kim raced ahead to the car and called Dina's foster parents, who agreed to meet them at the hospital.

Ethan set Dina gently in the backseat. Kim climbed in beside her and wrapped an arm around the girl. "Everyone was so worried about you," she said as Dina drifted into consciousness.

Dina's eyes rolled back in their sockets and then jerked forward.

Ethan pulled onto the main road. The interior light faded. Ethan flicked on the override, and his worried gaze caught Kim's in the rearview mirror. "Is she okay?"

"I don't know. Just hurry."

Dina started to say something, but the words came out garbled.

"Shush, honey. Don't try to talk. We'll get you to the hospital," Kim soothed.

The second Ethan parked outside the E.R., Dina's foster parents ran to the car and pulled Dina into their arms. A nurse coaxed them to release her into a wheelchair, then whisked her inside.

Kim looked at Ethan, feeling a little stunned at how quickly Dina was removed from their care.

"I'm sure they'll have questions for us," he said. "I'll park in the main lot, and we can join them inside."

As Ethan's urgent touch guided her through the parking lot, something inside her gave way. He was here to stop the flow of drugs so girls like Dina wouldn't end up in the hospital.

Or worse. The morgue.

And she had to tell him her brother was in on it.

Ethan rushed Kim inside only to find himself pacing the hallway waiting for word on Dina's condition. The toxicology report would take a while, but he suspected someone had slipped a roofie into her drink. Crack didn't do this. Neither did the marijuana some of her friends had to have been smoking. But she didn't appear to have been assaulted.

He slapped the wall. He needed to find out who sold her the drugs. He would've preferred to interrogate her in the car, away from curious ears, but the girl had been too disoriented.

"She'll be okay," Kim said, trailing him.

Right. One kid had already died on his watch. Now this.

Kim tugged on his arm. "Please, come and sit. I need to tell you something."

Ethan sat beside her, but inside he was still pacing, obsessing over how close he'd come to losing another kid. He sliced a sideways glance at Kim, noted the pinched whiteness of her lips, her hands twisted in her lap.

Without thinking, Ethan covered them with his own. Awareness jolted through him and he fought the instinct to draw back. Some things were more important than self-preservation.

"Hey, you just told me she's going to be okay. Why the long face?"

Kim's tormented gaze sucked the air from his lungs. "I—"

A shadow fell across their joined hands, and whatever she'd been about to tell him froze on her lips. Darryl looked down at them, a panicked urgency darkening his eyes.

Kim's face blanched. "Is Dad okay?"

Ethan's heart squeezed at the anguish in her voice, as he realized there was little other reason why her brother would traipse down here in the middle of the night. Except...

Ethan glanced at the window. It wasn't night anymore. Outside, the soft purple-gray of predawn light had already pushed away the darkness.

Darryl's gaze flicked to Ethan and back to Kim. "You need to come."

Kim sprang to her feet. "What happened?"

"You need to come. Now."

Kim's eyes narrowed, but before Ethan could figure out what *wasn't* being said, Dina's foster parents hurried toward them.

"How can we ever thank you?" Dina's foster mom exclaimed. "The doctor says Dina will be fine."

"May we speak to her?" Ethan asked.

"Yes, yes. She's asking for both of you. We're going to get her a sandwich." The woman beamed. "She says she's famished."

Kim, her expression torn, glanced from Dina's room to her brother.

Darryl caught her arm. "We need to talk."

"Excuse us a minute," Kim said to Ethan, and then pulled Darryl into the stairwell. "Why are you really here?"

"Have the police talked to you?"

"No. Why would they?" Her words echoed off the block walls.

"Because Dina's parents reported her missing, and you found her."

The real fear in Darryl's voice squeezed Kim's chest. He'd only wanted to spare their father more grief. He never could've imagined the domino effect of his actions. If he had...

Oh, if only he had.

"You can't tell them about me. They can't be trusted. Derk's got to have at least one cop in his back pocket. If he finds out I squealed..."

"You think he'll come after you?"

His remorse-filled gaze clung to hers for a moment before dipping to the floor. "It's a possibility."

"Darryl, a girl almost died today. We have to expose this man."

"Please, just give me a little more time."

She couldn't do that. It was bad enough that she hadn't told Ethan the moment they'd handed over Dina's care. But he'd been so distracted, she'd struggled to find the words. "I promise I won't say anything to a cop I don't know," Kim said. "But that's all I'll promise. Now, how's Dad, really?"

Darryl let out a resigned sigh. "The same."

"Okay, then I need to see Dina."

Kim rejoined Ethan outside Dina's room, but ignored the question in his eyes. Her news could wait a few more minutes.

Dina sat up as they entered.

"You're feeling better, huh?" Kim moved to her side.

Dina ducked her head. "Yes, thank you for finding me."

Kim smiled and motioned to Ethan. "This is the guy you need to thank."

"A promise that you'll never touch drugs again is all the thanks I want."

Dina held up her hand Girl Scout-style. "Oh, I promise. I can't believe my so-called friends just left me there after I passed out."

"Who gave you the drugs?" Ethan asked, giving the impression that the question was born of casual curiosity.

Kim knew better.

"A guy in my class." She snorted. "That other kid's death should've been my first clue the stuff was crap. I can't believe I was so dunce."

"This guy in your class, he have a name?" Ethan pressed, unwilling to speculate whether it was the drug she bought or something else.

The girl looked away.

Kim rubbed the girl's arm. "Honey, you need to tell us."

"If I snitch, the kids at school will make my life miserable."

"I promise no one will know," Ethan said. "I just want to talk to him, find out his supplier, get this pipeline turned off."

"Are you a cop or something?"

To spare Ethan from having to lie, Kim said, "Ethan works with me at Hope Manor. We want to keep other kids from ending up there."

"Or worse," Ethan added.

Dina's gaze darted to the door and back to them. "His name is Ryan Adams."

Kim gasped. "Adams? As in Lieutenant Adams?"

"Yeah, his son."

"Who's Lieutenant Adams?" Ethan asked.

"A cop whose reputation the papers smeared a couple of years back by circulating rumors of his connection to a pyramid scheme. The allegations were never proven."

Ethan's eyes brightened. "And you're sure this Ryan kid is the lieutenant's son?" When Dina nodded, Ethan's expression slowly transformed as if pieces of the puzzle were connecting in his mind.

But she still held the biggest piece. Kim's heart pummeled her rib cage. She had to tell him. As much as she didn't want to, she had to.

But how did she do that without destroying her family?

SIXTEEN

As quickly as he could, Ethan wrapped up their visit with Dina and excitedly ushered Kim out of the room. "We've found our dirty cop," he whispered in her ear.

"You shouldn't jump to any—" Kim's head turned, bringing her face within inches of his.

Ethan's heart rate kicked up for a whole different reason than excitement over the breakthrough. Had Kim's eyes always had so many intriguing flecks of color?

"This is the young man I was telling you about." Joy's cheery voice rang through the hall. The dark-haired gentleman pushing her wheelchair smiled indulgently. A gold band encircled his third finger, and for the first time Ethan noticed a matching one on Joy's.

Ethan blinked. "You're married?"

"Yes. I thought you knew," Joy exclaimed. "This is my husband, Blaine."

Ethan shook the man's offered hand. *Joy was married.*

A constriction in his chest he hadn't been aware of loosened and he took a deep breath. Deeper than he could remember taking in a long, long time.

"Our daughter's visiting her grandma in room 308," Joy nattered on.

"You have a daughter, too?" Ethan struggled to tone down his surprise.

"Yes, a real sweetie. Blaine's first wife died when Sarah was an infant. We've been married almost six years now." Joy fluttered her hand. "But enough about me. Look at you two. I knew the first time I saw you together you were smitten. Didn't I tell you that, Blaine?"

Blaine patted Joy's shoulder. "Yes, you did."

"I… We're not…" Kim spluttered, drawing a grin to Ethan's lips.

"Oh, hush now," Joy scolded. "Life's too short to deny what's as obvious as the nose on your face."

Kim's gaze shifted to Ethan and her cheeks bloomed into a gorgeous shade of pink.

Blaine turned Joy's chair. "Come, dear. You've embarrassed them enough."

Joy fluttered her fingers in a jovial wave and flashed them an unrepentant smile.

Hope bloomed in Ethan's chest. Feeling more lighthearted than he'd felt in years, he turned to share the newfound feeling with the woman he'd tried so unsuccessfully to resist.

But one look at Kim's face made his heart run cold. He knew that look. The look of a cop who had to deliver the worst news a person could hear.

He didn't need it spelled out to him. Just because she'd urged him to take to heart the youth pastor's message the other night didn't mean she was interested in him romantically. She was just being Kim—kind, compassionate and caring.

"Ethan, I—"

"Forget about it," he said, more sharply than he'd intended. "Joy's just being Joy. I'm not looking for a relationship, so go ahead and breathe."

"No, you misunderstood."

"I said forget it. You don't owe me an explanation. I'm not the kind of guy you'd want to get involved with."

Kim stared at him in shocked silence. She'd been so preoccupied with how to tell him about Darryl that she hadn't known how to react to Joy's observations about them. Except to know deep down in her heart that they were absolutely true.

If only things could've been different.

"I've got to talk to the chief," Ethan said, heading for the exit once again.

"Wait. I need to tell you something." She couldn't let the wrong guy get in trouble.

Then again, Lieutenant Adams might be exactly the dirty cop Darryl was worried about. If only she knew for sure, maybe they could catch the real bad guys without getting Darryl in trouble. "You can't just assume Adams is dirty because his son's selling drugs. He may not even know what his son's doing."

"How can a police lieutenant not recognize the signs in his own son?"

"Parents don't want to believe that their kids would do something like that."

"They may not want to believe it, but most suspect. I need to go."

"No, wait." Kim caught his arm. At his impatient scowl, her pulse rocketed. She dropped her voice to a whisper. "I know who the person is."

"What?" He steered her toward the exit. "We'll talk in my car." His voice reverberated with barely controlled anger, and it occurred to her that he might assume she'd known about Darryl all along.

Ethan's grip on her arm wasn't the least bit forgiving. Visions of him storming into her father's hospital room and handcuffing Darryl in front of him cut off her breath. How had she let the situation come to this?

She stumbled. Ethan's hold kept her from falling, but he didn't slow his dogged pace.

Inside the car, the air was so hot and sticky, she couldn't

breathe. Ethan's expression was fierce. Not even the most belligerent residents looked at her so severely. Her heart cracked.

Ethan started the engine and turned on the air conditioner. "Okay, talk."

"My brother..." She felt as if she'd dived off Niagara Falls and was flailing in the water, on the brink of being sucked under. She drew in a deep breath. "My brother is the one recruiting residents."

A momentary widening of Ethan's eyes was the only hint of his surprise. "How long have you known?" His jaw clenched as though he fought to keep his tone even.

She dropped her gaze, unable to bear the disappointment in his. "I suspected a couple of days ago. But I didn't know for sure until just before you showed up at the house."

When Ethan didn't respond, she added, "I'm sorry. I know I should've told you right away, but we had to find Dina, and then..."

"Let me guess. You're telling me now because as soon as I talk to Ryan, or his lousy excuse for a father, I'll find out anyway?" The bitterness in Ethan's voice stung.

"No. I've been trying to tell you all night. I wouldn't keep this from you. I couldn't live with myself if someone else died and I could've prevented it."

A muscle in Ethan's cheek flinched. "Too bad your brother never felt the same."

"He did. But he didn't know who he could trust. Ethan, please, you've got to believe me. Darryl is not a bad person. A guy named Derk is blackmailing him. Years ago, my dad was Derk's partner in a botched robbery attempt." The whole story tumbled out, choppy and disjointed. "Mom begged Darryl to do what Derk said so Dad could die in peace. They planned to go to the police as soon as he died."

"It doesn't matter what they planned to do. What he did is illegal. At the very least, he's guilty of obstruction of justice and corruption of a minor."

The chill in Ethan's voice ripped through her like an Arctic blast. Her insides trembled uncontrollably. Ethan's disappointment—no, disgust—with her, for not coming forward sooner, hurt almost as much as her fear of what he'd do with the information now.

"Darryl's certain Derk has a guy inside, like you said."

"Lieutenant Adams?"

"Maybe. I don't know. But don't you see? This guy will know Darryl talked, and Derk's bound to retaliate."

"I can't cover up Darryl's role in this."

Kim clutched Ethan's arm. "But if Darryl helps you locate Derk, couldn't you keep his name out of this?" If Ethan cared for her at all, he'd understand why she wanted to protect her brother. Darryl had been foolish, but he'd acted out of love. She couldn't bear the thought of him behind bars. And his arrest would kill Dad on the spot.

Ethan stared through the windshield at the black clouds gathering over the hospital building. Kim's brother had cost three youths their lives by cooperating with this Derk guy, and she was still defending him!

"Since no one knows you're a cop, you can question Darryl without Derk realizing the police are on to him."

"What makes you think Darryl will talk to me?"

"I'll tell him he has no choice. That if he doesn't, he'll be arrested."

"That's not my call. I can't overlook your brother's crimes." After the way Curt had clammed up when he'd spotted Kim, and then hearing about Beanpole's you-don't-want-to-know comment, he should've guessed it was her brother.

"I know he has to pay for what he's done. But with his life? Don't you see? If you arrest him before you have Derk in custody, they'll kill him!"

Her broken expression tugged at the ragged edges of his anger and left him completely undone. "How often does Darryl see this guy? If Darryl cooperates, maybe we could give him a wire and record Derk's negotiations."

"Darryl's never met Derk. They've only talked on the phone."

"Then how is Darryl supposed to help me find him?"

"You could trace the call. Couldn't you?"

"Maybe. Assuming the guy calls."

"I think Derk might be the guy I saw in the black SUV, the one who scared off my purse snatcher."

"How do you figure?"

"If he hates my dad so much, he probably gets his kicks out of frightening me."

"He scared *off* your purse snatcher."

"Okay, that part doesn't make sense. But I saw him come out of Dad's room a few days before that. And Dad was really upset afterward."

"Why didn't you—" Ethan hauled his voice down to a growl. "Why didn't you tell me this sooner?"

"I didn't make the connection to anything happening at the manor the first time I saw him." She dropped her gaze. "After I saw him at the park with my purse snatcher I was afraid you'd think my dad had something to do with the drugs, too."

Yeah, he would've, but her lack of trust still irked. "Okay, we'll pull Derk's arrest photo and see if you can ID him. But I'll need more than Darryl's testimony if I'm going to make the charges stick."

"If Derk believes Darryl's still cooperating, he's bound to say something incriminating."

Ethan didn't miss the hopeful note in her voice. "Yeah, maybe." Ethan thumbed open his phone. "I need to tell the chief to get someone on Adams. And to pull his phone records and figure out where he's been sticking his nose, before *he's* tipped off that we're on to him, too."

Kim threw her arms around his neck. "Oh, thank you. Thank you."

He steeled himself against a rush of emotion and reminded himself that her embrace was nothing more than spontaneous appreciation. Because, the last person she'd want to hug was the man who intended to arrest her brother, and by default, expose her father's secrets.

Ethan clasped her arms and set her away from him. "Go see your father. I'll be up after I talk to the chief. I'll want to hear everything your brother knows."

As she walked into the hospital, Ethan scanned the parking lot. He felt as though every eye was on him, from the intern in the bottle-cap glasses lounging on a park bench—the one who'd been reading the same page of the newspaper for the past fifteen minutes—to the heavily made-up redhead collecting money at the parking kiosk. Any one of them could be an informant for this Derk person.

Ethan called the chief and filled him in on the latest developments, minus Darryl. The chief said he'd email Derk's photo and anything else he could find to Ethan's cell phone, and that he'd ask Rick Gray to investigate Adams. Recognizing the name as that of Kim's friend's husband, Ethan was satisfied that the wrong people wouldn't be tipped off. And since they didn't want to alert Lieutenant Adams to their suspicions, interrogating his boy would have to wait. Ethan made his way into the hospital.

He hovered at the door of Mr. Corbett's room. Kim's father lay with his upper body propped up, oxygen hooked under his nose. His translucent skin hung from his cheekbones and pooled at his jowls in overlapping folds that made him look ninety instead of fiftysomething.

Darryl sat next to the bed, one hand cupping his bowed head and the other resting on his dad's arm.

Unwelcome feelings of pity filled Ethan. He hardened his heart against them. Sure, Darryl had only wanted to protect his dying father. But three kids were dead.

Kim stood on the opposite side. She spoke brightly to her

father, and although he didn't open his eyes, his lips turned up, realigning his wrinkles.

A lump swelled in Ethan's throat. Kim's love for her father was undiminished despite the disturbing revelations about his past.

She exchanged a sorrow-filled glance with her brother and a pang of envy caught Ethan in the gut. Kim's loyalty to her family was remarkable. If his parents had stood by him as steadfastly, perhaps...

He shook his head. The past was better left where it was. Even if Kim could look past his mistakes, hoping she'd forgive him for destroying her family was too much to wish for.

Engrossed in watching Kim with her dad, Ethan didn't notice Mrs. Corbett until she touched his arm.

"Thank you for finding Dina. We're so grateful," she said, cradling his hand between hers.

Her warm welcome filled him with longing and made him hate what he had to do. "I was happy to help."

"Oh, Ethan, you're here," Kim said, her voice jittery.

Darryl darted a nervous glance from Ethan to Kim as their mother drew him to her husband's bedside.

"I'm afraid he isn't terribly alert today." She patted the man's hand. "Dear, this is the new staff member Kim was telling you about."

The man's face brightened even more than it had earlier, and for some reason, that made Ethan feel worse.

Who was he kidding? He knew exactly why he felt like something you'd scrape off your shoes. Here he was plotting to expose their secrets, while they welcomed him as a hero.

Kim lovingly stroked the hair from her father's face and then lifted her gaze to Ethan's. Her devotion to her father shone in her eyes. Her lips trembled into a wavering smile. A smile that didn't pretend to be happy about what she'd asked of him, yet reiterated her gratefulness to him.

Her trust gripped his emotions and wouldn't let go. Everything in him wanted to spare her family from more heartache.

But he couldn't compromise justice because he had feelings for the suspect's sister.

At 2:00 a.m. Kim walked the perimeter of the yard for the first nightly check. The spotlights reflecting off the clouds gave an eerie glow to the night sky. From somewhere in the blackness beyond the fence, a deep-throated croak made her jump.

Terrific. If she was startling at bullfrogs, she'd be a nervous wreck in no time. She tugged on the first lock to ensure it was secure, and then shone her flashlight on it to make sure it was Hope Manor's. A couple of years ago, a gang had cut the locks in the middle of the night and replaced them with their own. The switch went unnoticed, and the next day they'd had a jailbreak on their hands.

Tonight, the thought of who might get in—not who might get out—had her flashlight skittering from bush to fence to tree.

The grainy image of Derk that Ethan had shown her had been twenty-five years old. He'd had long hair and pierced ears, but otherwise had very generic features—no cleft chin, no beak nose, no telltale scar on his cheek. Cut the hair and lose the earrings and he'd look like the old guy at the video store or the guy hawking hot dogs at Harbor Park. Or the guy from the hospital. She couldn't be certain.

Her light beam flicked across the walls of the new workshop—the culmination of Dad's concerted efforts to bring in trade-skills training for the boys.

Her heart crunched. When Darryl's connection with the drug ring came out, the manor would never survive.

Lord, I don't understand why You've let all these things happen. I thought this was the work You wanted me to devote my life to.

A scripture whispered through her mind. *All things work to-gether for the good of those who love Him.* Except, she couldn't imagine what good God would bring from the ache gripping her heart. The instant she'd begged Ethan not to arrest Darryl, she'd wanted to bite back the words, sickened that she'd asked him to compromise his duty. But she'd panicked at the thought of Derk going after Darryl and of what Darryl's arrest would do to Dad.

Now she couldn't shake from her mind the pained look on Ethan's face when she'd thanked him.

Ethan had tried every angle he could think of to urge Darryl to talk. Nothing had worked. Finally, Ethan did what he should've done in the first place. Never mind that Kim would probably never speak to him again. Darryl had left him with no choice but to break cover and haul him down to the police station.

Taunted by Kim's thank-you, Ethan paced the stuffy inter-rogation room, while Darryl sat as mutely as he had before his arrest.

"I want to help you," Ethan said for the hundredth time.

"Doesn't matter. I'm not talking."

"Look, for Kim's sake, I've viewed your involvement in this whole affair as coerced, but I *will* see you prosecuted to the full extent of the law if you don't start cooperating."

"You don't get it," Darryl exploded. "I don't care about myself. I deserve whatever's coming to me. But if I talk, Derk's threatened to…" Darryl's voice broke.

"To what?" Ethan demanded, getting in Darryl's face.

"Hurt Kim!" Darryl's hands fisted. "He sent Blake to run her off the road. The call I got that morning—that was him. He said if I didn't cooperate, next time the car wouldn't miss."

Images—stomach-turning snapshots of female victims—paraded through Ethan's mind. And ripped a hole through his chest.

Was this how Darryl felt every breathing moment?

Ethan hauled in a breath. "Why didn't you tell Kim she was in danger?"

Darryl slammed his fist on the table. "If Kim had so much as an inkling of why I refused to go to the police, she would have been at the station in a heartbeat. She won't risk the lives of others to protect herself."

"But you will?"

"To protect her. Wouldn't you?"

Ethan jerked back. Around Kim, he couldn't seem to keep his head. Every once in a while, in the middle of playing Ping-Pong or shooting hoops with the residents, he'd look up and find her watching him. And for a moment, he'd lose himself in the sparkle of her eyes, the way they crinkled at the corners when she smiled. Would he do anything to protect her?

Yeah.

Ethan straddled the chair facing Darryl. "Tell me where to find this guy, and I'll make sure he never lays a finger on Kim. In the meantime, she's safe at the manor. No one's getting in or out. And—" Ethan checked his watch "—in a few minutes, I'll head over there myself to pick her up. We'll put her into protective custody."

"No!" Darryl's gaze snapped from Ethan to the two-way mirror behind him. "Derk will know. He's got eyes everywhere."

Half asleep, Kim stood at the glass doors of Hope Manor's main entrance and watched for the school board's white utility van. With only three other staff on duty this early in the morning, she, as acting supervisor—and the only scheduled staff member with a key to the exits—had to meet the school-board courier and escort him to the classroom. He came every weekday morning to exchange a bag of GED exams and test packets with the one the teacher set aside for him.

Once he left, she only needed to brief the incoming shift,

and then she could finally call Ethan and find out if he'd caught Derk. She had to admit that he'd responded to her revelation about Darryl better than she'd hoped. She'd half expected him to haul her brother to jail on the spot. His willingness to hold off took a bit of the sting out of his disappointment with her.

The blush of morning tinted the sky above the trees. Kim glanced at her watch. Five thirty-five. The courier was late.

Kim rested her head against the door and closed her eyes. Somewhere along the line she'd gone from wanting to help Ethan find peace with his past to wanting him in her future, which made his disappointment in her hurt way more than it should. Unlike Nate, with Ethan, she felt cherished and valued and safe.

A rumbling motor rattled the glass door. She lifted her head with a start.

A van with the school board's logo pulled to the curb.

Kim pushed open the door, her mind still on Ethan. The ache in her heart intensified. She wasn't sure how it had happened, but in three short weeks, she'd fallen in love—in *love!*—with a man who, by his own choice, seemed determined to be alone.

The driver approached, cap pulled low over his face. Staff never asked for ID. After all, the guy drove a school-board van. But something about the way he clutched the red vinyl pouch seemed off.

Kim yanked the door back.

The guy caught it and, wedging his body through the opening, drilled her with familiar beady eyes.

The guy from the hospital. His eyes just like those in the photo. *Derk's!*

Kim fumbled for the button on her walkie-talkie.

Derk kicked it to the ground.

Backing toward the inner set of doors, she patted the air with her palms. "Take it easy. What do you want?"

He drew a gun from the bag, a silencer screwed to the end. "You."

SEVENTEEN

Derk pointed his gun at her heart, and Kim's scream froze in her throat.

Her gaze darted from door to door of the glass-enclosed entranceway. She was trapped. She'd never be able to fit her key into a lock fast enough to make a run for it. And at this range, he couldn't miss.

She didn't dare antagonize him. When she didn't return, someone would come looking for her. Except…as acting supervisor, she wasn't expected to return to a unit.

And the day staff wouldn't be in for another twenty minutes.

Somehow she had to stall him.

"Why—" she started to ask, but the word came out weak and quavery. Swallowing the terror balled in her throat, she tried again. "Why do you want me?"

"No questions."

A male voice came over her walkie-talkie. "Kim, I need you on unit two. ASAP. Over."

Injecting a calm she didn't feel into her voice, Kim said to Derk, "If I don't answer that call, staff will come looking for me. Is that what you want?"

He motioned the muzzle toward the walkie-talkie. "Tell him you'll be a few minutes. Nothing more." He chambered a bullet. "Understand?"

Her mind scrambled for a way to clue the staff into the emergency without alerting Derk.

Cautiously, she moved toward the walkie-talkie he'd kicked across the floor. If she used the word *now,* staff might recognize the standard emergency call. But dare she say where she was and risk his retaliation?

Derk caressed the trigger, and she trembled so badly she almost dropped the walkie-talkie. Depressing the talk button, she said, "I can't come *now.*" She paused for a fraction longer than needed. "I'll be a few minutes. Over."

Immediately, Kevin came back with, "Where are you?"

She pressed the talk button a second time, but as she opened her mouth, the butt of the gun hammered toward her head. Screaming, she ducked and tackled Derk like a linebacker going for the kill. The gun bounced off the bulletproof glass and raked across her back.

He flung her off him and she landed in a heap against the door.

She tried to rise, but her knees buckled.

Derk grabbed the gun, then her arm, and hauled her to her feet. "Open the door," he said, pushing her toward the exit.

Confused that he wanted out, not in, she fumbled with the keys, stalling as long as she dared, hoping someone would come, praying whoever did wouldn't be greeted by a hail of bullets.

Derk snatched the key ring from her hand, unlocked the door and shoved her out ahead of him. She cast a look toward the parking lot, but Darryl wasn't there yet.

No one was.

With one hand on her arm and the gun pressed to her back, Derk prodded her toward the van.

"Why are you doing this?"

"To teach your old man a lesson." He jerked her other arm behind her back.

Wait. That meant he must've pocketed the gun. She reared

to knock him off balance, but he might as well have been a stone wall.

He cinched her wrists tight. "Nice try." He shoved her into the back of the utility van.

Her shoulder bumped against something spongy. In the dim light she made out the outline of a body. She recoiled, screaming.

"Quiet or I'll do the same to you." Derk slammed the door.

The person on the floor of the van groaned. Kim walked on her knees to his side. The man's hands and feet were tied and he had a gag over his month. His panic-stricken eyes reached out to her. This had to be the courier whose van Derk had hijacked.

"If I'm the one you want, why don't you let this guy go?"

Derk laughed. "I'll give it to your old man. He sure raised a couple of bleeding hearts." Derk dragged open the side door, yanked the courier out and shoved him into the trees. Climbing into the driver's seat, Derk said, "When you see your dad, be sure and tell him what a nice guy I am. Unlike him." Derk snorted. "We were supposed to be friends. Did he tell you I took him in when his old man threw him out on the street? And how does he repay me?

"By forgetting me, that's how. He gets religion and pats himself on the back for his good deeds, but did he ever lift a finger to try to help me? No."

"But he didn't know what happened to you. Not until your case went to trial."

Derk shifted the van into gear. "If he hadn't let that bitty old woman out the bank door, I wouldn't have had to shoot the guard in the first place."

"You never had to shoot anyone." Bile scorched Kim's throat. How could this man ever have been Dad's friend?

She scanned the dim interior of the van for something she could use as a weapon. Derk had one hand on the wheel and one hand on the gun in his lap. She didn't dare try to knock him out while they were moving. If he lost control of the van, she'd be mincemeat. But if she could catch him off guard the next time he stopped at an intersection, she might be able to make a run for it.

"I wanted your old man to see what it felt like to be betrayed," Derk went on. "I never expected your brother to play along. But I gotta admit, corrupting the preacher-warden's son was the sweetest irony."

Kim winced at the sick pleasure in the man's voice. His thirst for revenge had driven him beyond reason. This was the kind of guy Ethan dedicated his life to taking off the street. No wonder he'd been furious that she hadn't divulged her suspicions of Darryl sooner. And even before that, how could she have thought it was okay not to admit that the guy in the SUV had been to see her dad?

Ethan had a job to do—an important job—and she'd compromised it. If she'd confided in him immediately, this creep might already be behind bars.

"Yup, this sleepy town has been lucrative. That's for sure. Too bad your brother couldn't keep his mouth shut." Derk slammed on the brakes.

Kim toppled face-first into the metal ridges of the floor. Her tongue pinched between her teeth and pain rocketed through her mouth. She tasted blood.

"Now I'll have to move on and set up shop somewhere else." Derk accelerated again.

Kim's chin raked across the gritty floor. Rolling onto her side, she curled into a ball and tried to bring her tied hands under her feet to her front. The van veered around a corner, driving her into a sidewall. She braced herself against it and worked her way back up to her knees. What now?

With her hands anchored behind her back, she'd never be able to swing a weapon hard enough to be effective. And without having her arms for balance, she doubted she'd be able to kick the back of his head. Escape was her only option.

If she could get the rear door open, she could drop out the next time the van slowed. Keeping her eyes on the rearview mirror, she edged toward the back of the van.

"Yup, by the time the police figure out where I live, I'll be long gone. But I couldn't leave without keeping my promise, now, could I?" he said, his voice syrupy.

Her brother's plea flashed through her mind. *This isn't about Dad anymore.* She gasped. Darryl knew. He knew Derk would come after her.

Derk's hollow gaze met hers in the rearview mirror. "Where's your God now, eh, girlie?"

"Beside me. Always," she said, defiantly.

Irrationally, her thoughts went to Ethan. Why hadn't she had the courage to tell him she loved him?

Derk snorted, and when his eyes returned to the road, Kim saw her chance. She craned her tied hands toward the door.

The van jerked to a stop.

Kim toppled, twisting her shoulder just in time to save her face from another meeting with the floor. She bit back a yowl of pain as she scrambled to regain her footing. From the corner of her eye, she saw Derk drive the stick shift into Park and grab his gun.

She got to her knees just as he swung it toward her.

"What do you think you're doing?"

Back pressed against the door, she reached blindly for the handle.

Derk's stocky frame blocked what little light she had as he rose and advanced toward her.

A hysterical scream caught in her throat. She couldn't breathe. She didn't want to die. Not here. Not like this. Straining against the ties cinched around her wrists, she tried desperately to work the lock.

Derk grabbed her chin and dug his fingers into her cheeks. "I said, what do you think you're doing?"

Tears filled her eyes. *Please, Lord, save me.*

The latch gave and the door fell open, taking her with it. The instant of euphoria ended the moment her back hit the pavement. The air whooshed from her lungs. Gravel bit into her spine. She faced the sky, blue and endless, but the smell of exhaust overpowered the smell of freedom.

Her thoughts returned to Ethan. *Lord, if this is my time, please don't let Ethan blame himself,* she prayed.

And the last thing she saw was the butt of Derk's gun spearing toward her head.

Late. Ethan swerved onto the drive that wound down the hill to the manor, grinding into second gear. He shot a glance at the parking lot. No sign of Kim yet.

Whoa. Was that a foot?

He braked sharply, his heart clenching with dread.

Pulling his gun, he slipped out the passenger door and used the car for cover. He pointed his gun at the roadside foliage.

"Police, come out with your hands up."

A muffled groan rose from the clutch of goldenrod and long grasses.

"I said, come out with your hands up," Ethan repeated, scanning the vicinity for signs of a sniper.

A bound and gagged man struggled into view, but Ethan couldn't be sure that he wasn't being baited. He edged around the car, every sense on high alert.

The man wrestled to his knees, his eyes pleading for help.

Ethan moved in low and swift and dragged the man into the backseat of the car, then tore the duct tape from the his mouth.

"He's got the girl," the man yelled.

Ethan's stomach dropped to his knees. "What girl?"

"From the manor. I'm the school-board courier. Some guy stole my van and then kidnapped a girl."

"Can you describe her?" Ethan asked, knowing the answer. Brown hair, ponytail, green eyes, five-six. Kim. He could hardly breathe around the lump in his throat.

Using his pocketknife, he sliced through the binds on the man's wrists and ankles. "How long ago?" The thought of Kim in danger felt like a bullet, point-blank to the center of his chest.

"Twenty minutes."

Ethan whipped out a notepad and pen. "I need a full description of your assailant and the van he stole." With a twenty-minute head start, Derk could have Kim out of the region by now, or holed up who knew where.

"I didn't see his face, but the van's a white cargo. School-board logo on the side. License plate WODE 210."

Ethan pulled out his phone and relayed the information to the chief. "We can't wait on wiretaps now. You're gonna have to haul Lieutenant Adams in. Find out what he knows. Put Darryl on."

"I told you this would happen," Darryl ranted into the phone. "This is all your fault."

"You listen to me," Ethan said. "If you want me to find your sister alive, I need to know everything you know about this guy."

"Like I told you before, all I know is he did twenty-five years for murder. Got out three years ago. Name was Derk Vance."

Was being the operative word. A quick search had turned up nothing on the name—no car, no home, no credit cards or bank accounts. "So he'd be around fifty?"

"Mom figured closer to sixty."

"Okay. What else? Did you hear any background noise that might give us a clue where he called you from? Think. Kim's life could depend on it." As if to punctuate his words, sirens whirred in the distance.

"I saw a guy at the hospital one time that—"

"What did he look like?"

"Nothing like the news photos from the trial, but—"

"What did he look like, Darryl?"

"Short gray hair. Muscular build. My height. Expensive suit."

Sounded like the guy Kim suspected.

"Ethan," the chief interrupted. "I just got word the van's been located. It was abandoned ten kilometers east of town on Highway 3."

"He could be running for the border. Alert the highway patrol and the border guards."

"Already done."

Ethan's adrenaline surged. If Derk tried to cross the border with Kim, they had a fighting chance of stopping him. "Okay, while your men comb this place for evidence, I'm going to lean on that kid Zane you arrested for vandalizing Kim's car."

"He made bail." The chief relayed the kid's address.

"Okay, call me as soon as you've got Adams and his boy."

"You should know," the chief said, his voice grim. "There were signs of a struggle in the van and blood on the road outside the rear door."

Ethan steeled himself against the image that rose in his mind. He swallowed hard. He didn't need to know Kim was bleeding to know they were running out of time.

Slowly, Kim became conscious of movement, but she couldn't seem to pry open her eyes. An acrid smell seeped into her awareness. She tried to talk, but her tongue felt sluggish and too big in her dry mouth. The chair she was in *bump-bumped,* making her head loll forward and back and, try as she might, she couldn't seem to tell her brain to hold her head steady.

A bell dinged, and through slitted eyes she made out the blink of a circle of light. Her stomach jumped. How did she get here? And where was here? She tried to lift her hand, but a tight band gripped her wrist to the chair's armrest. Something soft brushed over her skin. Then hands roughly grazed her sides as if tucking a blanket around her.

"Where—" The word burned her throat, but only a moan escaped.

"You're waking up just in time," a harsh, vaguely familiar voice said.

What was wrong with her? Why couldn't she wake up?

Someone yanked her ponytail and her head snapped back against the seat. Her eyes popped open.

An older gentleman in a suit and tie smiled down at her, only his smile wasn't at all pleasant.

Her eyelids felt so heavy, her mind hazy. They seemed to be in a hospital elevator. And she was in a wheelchair. Good, because her head, her shoulder, every muscle in her body throbbed.

Suddenly, the events of the morning crashed through her consciousness. Derk! The scream surged up her throat, but no sound came out. Her scalp burned as her hair went taut. She felt as if, at any moment, it would be torn out by the roots.

"The drug paralyzes the vocal cords, among other things," he said with a chuckle. "We wouldn't want you screaming, now, would we?"

Terror welled inside her until its sheer volume should've caused it to burst from her mouth. But only the barest whimper reached her ears.

The elevator doors swished open, and Derk pushed her into a hallway. "Just sit back and enjoy the ride," he said, his voice vibrating with feverish zeal. "I know I will."

Dimly, Kim recognized the posters on the walls. Posters she'd walked past every day for the past few weeks. And a new terror gripped her.

They were going to Dad's hospital room. Was Derk so demented that he'd force her father to watch him kill her?

She tried to swing her head to attract someone's attention, but he clutched her hair too tightly. Voices drifted from the nurse's station at the other end of the hall, but Derk didn't have to pass the desk to reach Dad's room. Kim strained against the bindings on her arms and legs, but they were so tight her fingers had started to go numb. Or was that from the drug, too?

Derk inched his fingers deeper into her hair, pulling her gaze to his. "Sit still like a good girl," he cooed, his lips twisting into a sadistic sneer. He pushed the wheelchair into Dad's room and shut the door behind them.

Derk positioned her at the end of the bed and then cranked up the other end.

Oh, no, did he intend to kill Dad, too? Crazed with fear, she fought all the harder against her restraints.

Awakened by the bed's movement, Dad struggled to throw off the grip of sleep, and there was nothing she could do to save him. Or herself.

Like a faded movie, dreams of getting married and holding her first child flickered through her mind. Dreams that, since Nate's betrayal, she'd pretended weren't important. Dreams that she'd let flit momentarily through her heart after Ethan's kiss, only to bury them all the deeper after learning why he was really here.

Except now all she could remember were the dozens of ways he'd tried to protect her. And more than anything she wished she'd told him she loved him.

Derk yanked open the blinds.

The light stabbed Kim's eyes, sending shockwaves through her already-pounding head.

"Wakey, wakey," Derk singsonged. "It's time to say goodbye."

EIGHTEEN

Ethan clenched his fingers into a fist and pounded on Zane's door a third time. "Open up. Police." What was the judge thinking, granting this punk bail? Any parentless eighteen-year-old who could raise that kind of cash had to be selling drugs.

The inside door jerked open. Zane peered out the screen door, yawning and rubbing his eyes. "What's going on?"

Ethan pushed his way into the house. "Where'd your boss take Kim Corbett?"

Zane's gaze drilled into him. "I don't know what you're talking about. I don't work for nobody."

"Why else would you back off when he ordered you to drop the purse you already had in your grubby fist?" Ethan pulled a pair of cuffs from his back pocket. "We can do this the easy way or we can do it the hard way."

Zane's hands shot up. "Whoa, man. I'm tellin' ya, you've got the wrong guy." His gaze shot sideways as if he intended to bolt.

Ethan grabbed Zane by the arm and twisted it behind his back. "Yeah? Mind telling me what you were doing in his black SUV? We know he paid you to threaten Kim Corbett."

"You mean the dude in the suit? He paid me to *not* mess with her. Said he had other plans for her. Gave me fifty bucks."

Ethan's gut wrenched. "What plans?"

"I don't know. He didn't tell me."

Ethan snapped on a cuff. "No?"

"Hey. There's no law against taking money to leave someone alone."

"I'm not taking you in for taking his money. I'm taking you in for conspiracy to kidnap, and if we don't find Kim alive, accessory to murder."

"What?" Zane twisted against Ethan's hold. "I don't know nothin' about a kidnapping."

Ethan snapped on the other cuff, turned Zane around, grabbed the collar of his shirt and got into his face. "Something tells me the judge won't see it that way."

"I'm tellin' you. You've got the wrong guy."

"Then tell me where I can find the right guy."

"Get real. A dude like that's not gonna tell a guy like me where he lives."

Frustration ripped through Ethan's chest. Every second lost could be Kim's last. He should've gone for Kim the minute Darryl told him about Derk's threats. He should've listened to her in the first place and never arrested her brother. What good had it done him?

None. None at all.

He tightened his grip on the kid's shirt, letting his stop-at-nothing resolve blaze from his eyes. "Tell me what you *do* know."

The kid paled. "He s-said…" Zane stuttered and looked away.

"What?" Ethan gave him a shake, forcing his mind to stay focused on the kid and not imagine what Derk could be doing to Kim. "What did he say?"

"He wanted to teach her old man a lesson."

The hospital.

Ethan unsnapped the kid's cuffs and raced from the house, praying he wasn't too late.

* * *

Kim strained against the duct tape clamping her to the wheelchair as Derk zip-tied Dad's wrists to the bed rails.

Dad was groggy from being awakened from a medicated sleep and didn't seem to realize anything was wrong.

Derk cuffed him across the cheek, and tears sprang to Kim's eyes. "I said *wake up*." Derk shoved Kim's wheelchair up to the bed. "Don't you want to say goodbye to your precious daughter?"

Dad's eyes fluttered once, twice, and then finally stayed open. He looked about in confusion, but when his gaze settled on hers, a warm smile curved his lips. "Kimmy," he whispered.

Kim tried to smile, but the drug slackening her muscles made it feel like a grotesque imitation of the real thing. Tears streamed down her cheeks, and she couldn't even raise her hand to wipe them away.

Dad seemed to have a peculiar kind of tunnel vision that only saw her in the room. "Kim, what's wrong?"

She tried to answer, but managed nothing more than an indecipherable grunt.

"I'm afraid she can't talk right now," Derk gloated. He drew out a long, lethal-looking knife. Sunlight glinted off the blade. Slowly, as if savoring the way she froze at his touch, he stroked the blade's tip across her bottom lip. "But if you'd prefer to hear her screams, that can be arranged."

Dad lurched forward, only to be ricocheted back by the pull of his tied arms. His breath came in short gasps, and Kim guessed his physical pain was as acute as his emotional. "Who are you? What do you want?"

"I'm hurt that you don't remember me, old pal. Don't you remember my visits?"

As if Derk had pulled a plug, the panicked rage drained from Dad's face. The emotion that replaced it looked eerily familiar. She'd seen it in Ethan's eyes. Guilt.

"Ah, so you do remember me, I see. As for what I want—" Derk stroked his fingers through Kim's hair, and when she jerked away, he laughed maliciously. "I want payback."

Dad's fingers groped for the call bell. "I'm sorry I left you. I'll…I'll make it up to you. Please, just don't hurt my family."

A wicked gleam lit Derk's eyes. "Should you tell him, or shall I?" he said to Kim, and then laughed at his sick joke when her screaming retort dribbled out as a pathetic whimper.

"Right, I'd better tell him." His beady eyes fixed on Dad. "Your offer is too little too late, old pal. I chose to exact my pound of flesh another way."

Derk clamped his hand on her head.

Kim's breath caught. She shrank back, her gaze riveted on the knife. He was going to cut her. Here. Now. In front of Dad. *No, Lord, please protect me.*

Derk tilted her head sideways and caressed the blade down her cheek and throat.

Blinding fear rushed over her.

His lips curved wickedly. "I figured it's only fair that you should experience what I felt—despised and betrayed by those closest to you."

"Please," Dad pleaded. His fingers caught the cord of the call bell and inched the button toward his hand.

Kim held her breath, terrified that Derk would notice, too.

"Don't make Kim pay for my mistake," Dad went on.

Derk ripped the cord from Dad's hand and yanked the other end from the wall. "Haven't you read your Bible, preacher boy? Children pay for the sins of their fathers." Derk pressed the tip of his knife into Kim's cheek.

A scream of pain surged up her throat.

"Stop," Dad cried out. "What do you want from me?"

"You're not listening. I…want…you…to…suffer. You sit in your ivory tower and pretend you're this perfect person. But tell me, what kind of person abandons their friend in his hour of need?"

Kim's thoughts veered to Ethan. By now, he must know Derk had kidnapped her. He'd torture himself for not preventing it. If she didn't survive, he'd never forgive himself. Never.

And it was all her fault.

Dad's face turned even more ashen as Derk delighted in detailing how he'd corrupted Darryl into recruiting drug pushers.

His anguish tore at her heart until she didn't think she could hurt any worse. She'd utterly failed him. She wished she'd never been born.

"Don't ever think that," Dad said fiercely.

Kim's gaze snapped to his. Was he talking to her or Derk?

Tears clung to her father's eyelashes. As if he'd read her mind, he whispered, "Kimmy," and she felt herself enfolded in the warmth of his love. "God always has a plan." Dad's eyes slipped shut. His body stilled.

No!

Ethan raced up the stairs two at a time to the hospital's fourth floor. The ward was in chaos. Doctors and nurses rushed past and disappeared into room twelve.

Kim's father's room.

Ethan's pulse roared in his ears as he skidded to a stop outside the door.

"Time of death, six forty-five," the doctor said solemnly.

A moan ripped from Ethan's throat.

A nurse lifted the blanket over Mr. Corbett's face. "Look at this, doctor. His hands have been tied to the bed rails."

Ethan plowed into the room, flashing his badge. "Did anyone see a man and woman leave this room?"

"Not exactly," one of the nurses spoke up. "But I noticed a well-dressed gentleman pushing a woman in a wheelchair toward the elevator."

Ethan raced for the stairwell, shouting over his shoulder that they were not to touch the body until an evidence team cleared the room. Hurtling down the stairs, he called the chief and updated him on the situation.

"We haven't been able to locate Adams," the chief said. "His wife claims he left for the gym at five-thirty. His shift started ten minutes ago, so if he doesn't show soon, we'll have to assume he knows we're on to him."

"And that he's listening to the police scanner to help Derk stay one step ahead of us," Ethan added. By the time he hit the exit, his lungs were burning. He scanned the parking lot for a black SUV—something he should've done when he arrived.

Metal clanking on pavement sounded to his right. An overturned wheelchair with duct tape clinging to its armrests.

Drawing his weapon, Ethan ran toward it.

In the distance, sirens screamed. Then sounds of a struggle erupted behind the Dumpsters. A man cursed vilely.

His heart in his throat, Ethan stepped into view.

A man fitting Derk's description drove a blood-tipped knife straight for Kim's head.

Ethan trained his gun on the guy's back. "Drop the knife."

At the same time, Kim grabbed Derk's arm with both hands, locked her elbows and braced herself against the side of the SUV. But her experience with physical restraints was no match for a 240-pound man.

Ethan closed the distance, his gun leveled on Derk's back, looking for a shot that wouldn't go clear through into Kim.

Derk drove the knife toward the SUV, wrenching Kim's arms over her head. He scooped his free arm around her waist and pulled her away from the vehicle. In an instant, he was behind her, shielded by her body and dangerously close to breaking her hold.

Kim's arms shook viciously under the strain. Her eyes reached out to Ethan, screaming for him to do something. Any second her elbows would snap and the downward force of Derk's arm would drive the knife into her back.

Rage exploded inside him. He charged toward them and

speared the muzzle of his gun into the base of Derk's throat. "I said, drop the knife."

Derk's hand immediately opened. The knife glanced off Kim's shoulder and fell harmlessly to the ground.

Kim released her grip on Derk's arm and sprang away from him.

Police cars swerved to a stop, blocking them in on three sides. Doors swung open and officers crouched behind them, guns trained on Ethan. "Drop the weapon!"

"I'm a police officer. This is the kidnapper," he shouted, long past caring whether he worked undercover ever again. "Tell them, Kim!"

Her words spilled out barely audible, let alone comprehensible.

"I tried to stop him, officers!" Derk drowned out her explanation, looking too believable in his fancy suit with a gun at his neck. "He was trying to shove this poor girl into his vehi—"

With a growl, Ethan dug the gun deeper into the hollow of Derk's throat.

"Drop your weapon," the officer in charge repeated.

"Look at the description in your BOLO alert, people," Ethan said. "This is the kidnapper we've been hunting for the past hour." This was an undercover cop's worse nightmare. He had no idea what the code or color of the day was to prove he was one of them. And he had no intention of letting go of Derk until Kim was safely out of harm's way. "Get Kim out of here."

A fourth police car careened in alongside the others. The driver jumped from the car and aimed his gun at Ethan.

They locked gazes.

Adams. He had to be. Ethan dragged in a calming breath. If he didn't play this right, Adams would take him out and make it look like an accident.

Kim went ballistic. "No," she screamed, finally finding her voice. She flailed her arms, charging closer to danger instead of farther away.

"Kim, get back," Ethan shouted.

An officer broke cover and grabbed her, but she scratched and clawed and kicked, her gaze fixed on Ethan.

"Get her out of there," Adams ordered.

With Kim stowed safely behind a police car, Ethan lifted his gun from Derk's neck and pointed it skyward in surrender.

"Place it on the ground," Adams said, then muttered into his mouthpiece.

Ethan half squatted to drop his weapon, his other hand still firmly gripping Derk's collar.

Kim's gaze bucked to Adams taking a bead on him, and Ethan's heart stopped as she charged back into the line of fire.

Derk reached into his pocket.

Fear, sharper than he'd ever tasted, slashed Ethan's throat. "Get down," he screamed.

Shouts of "Gun, gun," erupted from behind the line of police cars.

Ethan elbowed Derk's gun arm.

A shot cracked the air. Return fire ripped through the side of the SUV. Windows shattered, showering them with glass.

Heat blazed across Ethan's shoulder. He pushed Derk to the dirt and wrestled the gun from his grip.

"Cease fire!" an officer shouted.

Kim lay face up on the tarmac, her face white, blood staining the front of her shirt.

Icy terror clutched Ethan's chest. He scrabbled to her side and pressed his palm to her wound. "Get a gurney out here!"

He brushed the hair from her face and put his mouth to her ear. "Hang on, Kim. You're going to be okay."

Her eyes fluttered, but didn't open.

Blood, too much blood, seeped through his fingers.

"Do you hear me, Kim? You're going to be okay." *Oh, God, please let her be okay.*

Two hospital attendants rushed over with a gurney. An officer hauled Ethan to his feet and slapped on cuffs.

"I can't leave her!"

The officer dragged him out of the way. And as Kim disappeared through the E.R. doors, Ethan's heart felt as if it was being ripped from his chest.

NINETEEN

Ethan lashed free of the officer's grip, searing pain flaming down his arm. Sure, he deserved to rot in prison for what he'd let happen to Kim, but if this cop expected to put him there before he saw her, he'd have to shoot him again.

"Uncuff him. He's one of ours," Chief Reynolds ordered, striding toward them.

"About time you showed up," Ethan ground out.

"Good work, Ethan. We got phone records connecting Adams and Derk. We're taking them in now."

"How's Kim? Any word? I've got to go to her."

"Get your own wound patched up first."

Ethan cupped his shoulder. "It's just a scratch."

"Then it won't take long to treat."

Twenty minutes later Ethan headed to the surgical floor. He caught sight of Joy outside the waiting room. "How's Kim?"

Joy's compassionate expression cut him off at the knees. "She needs our prayers, Ethan. She's lost a lot of blood, and every minute more they spend probing around in there..." Tears filled Joy's eyes. "They're doing everything they can."

Ethan slumped against the wall. "This is all my fault."

"You aren't to blame. You got her away from that awful man."

"It wasn't enough." The image of Kim stepping in front of

Adams's gun swiped his breath. "What does God want from me? 'Cause I'll do anything—*anything*—to save her."

"He wants you to trust Him. That's all He's ever wanted."

"She doesn't deserve to pay for my mistakes." Ethan lifted his head and forced his gaze to meet Joy's. "It's bad enough that you've had to."

"Bargaining with God for Kim's life is as much a lack of faith as hanging on to your guilt over something you've long since been forgiven for."

His heart pounded as images of Joy's accident flashed before his eyes like unwanted snapshots torn from a battered scrapbook—the car speeding beside him, the bend in the road, the roar of laughter, the sun glaring through the windshield, the thud of metal against flesh.

A rueful, agonized sound burned his throat.

"Circumstances don't always go 'our' way, Ethan. This wheelchair is proof of that. But God's love and grace exist no matter what happens. You need to believe that. Kim needs you to believe that. Because God loves Kim more than you ever could."

He reached for Joy's hand, squeezed it. Dropped it back in her lap. And then reached for it again.

"Oh, God," Ethan whispered, closing his eyes against the taunts of *Why would He listen to you?* screaming in his head. "I want to believe. I don't deserve Your mercy. But Kim does. Spare her, Lord. Please."

Joy's hand tightened around his. "Why can't you see that by clinging to your remorse, you're strangling the joy God wants you to have?"

Ethan's gaze snapped to hers. "Kim asked me that once."

"And what did you tell her?"

"That I didn't want to talk about it."

Joy gave him an understanding smile. "Do you love Kim?"

Did he love her? He loved that she wasn't afraid to stand up to him. He loved her refusal to give up on the kids at the manor. He loved that she'd trusted him enough to let him do his job even though it threatened everything she'd worked for.

Yes, he loved her. The word hardly seemed big enough to describe how he felt about her. And it terrified him.

Kim may not have rejected him for his past, but he'd arrested her brother and endangered her life, not to mention likely destroyed her chances of saving Hope Manor. If she lived, how could she bear to look at him now, let alone return his feelings?

"Ethan?"

"Yes." His voice cracked. "I love her."

"You love her so much you'd forgive her anything?"

"Yes, anything." He palmed the moisture pooling under his eyes.

"Could you forgive her for behaving recklessly and injuring someone you care about?"

"She'd never—"

"But if she did, could you forgive her?"

"Yes. I love her."

"I don't think you took enough time to really consider my question. What if you had a child, and in Kim's haste, she accidentally backed into him with her car? Could you forgive her then?"

"How could you ask such a horrible thing?"

"Could you forgive her?"

He hesitated. "I'd be angry. Devastated. But yes, knowing how utterly tormented she'd feel, I'd do anything to help her find peace."

"You'd forgive her?"

"Yes! I already told you."

"Ethan, God loves you more than you could ever love Kim. Why is it so hard for you to believe He's forgiven you?"

Ethan's breath caught in his chest. Put in that light, every possible reason why God could never forgive him fled his mind. He closed his eyes and prayed with renewed vigor.

A nurse exited the O.R. and walked toward the room where Mrs. Corbett and Darryl, who'd been granted permission on compassionate grounds to be with her, awaited news of Kim.

Ethan and Joy rushed over.

Mrs. Corbett looked as though she'd aged ten years in the past twenty-four hours. She'd lost her husband, and now…

Ethan braced his hand on the door frame. "Mrs. Corbett, I'm sorry for your loss and for—"

Darryl's gaze bucked to his. "Get out! You're not welcome here. I told you Derk would get to her. I told you!"

"Darryl," Mrs. Corbett said sharply. "This is our fault, not Ethan's. He saved her."

Ethan's insides crumbled at the unmerited reprieve.

Mrs. Corbett's red-rimmed eyes held his for a long moment. "I would've given anything to take my husband's place. I can see you feel the same about Kim." She returned her attention to the nurse. "How is she?"

The nurse's gaze flicked from Mrs. Corbett to them, and then back to Mrs. Corbett, who waved her hand. "They're fine."

"Her bowel's been nicked. The surgery could go on for some time yet. The risk of infection is high, and she has little strength left."

"Then she needs our prayers more than ever," Joy said, reaching for Ethan's hand.

Ethan clasped Mrs. Corbett's hand, who covered Darryl's with her other. Darryl closed the circle by taking Joy's. Ethan prayed as if his life depended on it. And it just might, because Kim was the one person who made him feel truly alive.

Yet, even knowing that God's answer might be no, a new sense of peace came over him.

They prayed and prayed, and then sat in silence as the minute hand circled the clock.

At some point Joy had left to see other patients.

Finally, the doctor appeared at the door. "Mrs. Corbett?"

"Yes." She sprang to her feet.

Ethan felt himself start to hyperventilate and forced himself to take deep breaths. He couldn't lose it. Not now. Kim might need him.

"Your daughter has pulled through surgery and is in recovery."

Ethan swallowed a sob and let his eyes slip shut. *Thank You, Lord.*

When the nurse came to take the Corbetts to see Kim, she explained that only two visitors were permitted in the ICU at a time.

Ethan squeezed Mrs. Corbett's hand and sat back down.

To his surprise, Darryl stopped and shook his hand. "I'm sorry about what I said earlier."

"It's forgotten."

Darryl nodded, blinked away a tear. "Thank you for getting Kim away from Derk."

"You're welcome."

Alone in the waiting room, Ethan fought a wave of grief so powerful it threatened his newfound peace. "Oh, God, You spared Kim's life, but *I* could still lose her. Making peace with You doesn't mean she'll forgive me. I know that. And I won't bargain with You anymore. Just…"

Her smile rose to his mind. A smile that held him together when the world seemed to be falling apart.

"Oh, God, just give me strength."

Pain clawed at Kim's side, dragging her fuzzy brain from a strange, thick fog.

"Kim. Kim, can you hear me?" A cool hand enveloped hers.

She pried open her eyes and her pulse quickened. An IV dripped into her arm. Monitors crowded the space next to her. "What—? How long—?"

A nurse leaned into her line of vision. "You were shot."

Shot?

"You've been unconscious for twenty-seven hours." The nurse asked her a bunch of questions and checked her vitals.

Twenty-seven hours. The last thing she remembered was Dad—

Oh, no, Dad!

The nurse patted her arm. "You have a lot of people anxious to see you awake."

"Hi, honey," Mom said, giving Kim's hand a gentle squeeze. Her beaming smile almost made Kim forget the grief bruising her heart. Grief for Dad, and—

Memories of a gun swamped her. Followed by panic. "Ethan?"

"He's right here," Mom soothed, stepping aside.

"You had us worried," he said, his voice rough with emotion.

Something warm and wonderful swelled in her chest. "You're alive," she whispered.

Ethan cradled her hand in his. "I am now." He brought her hand to his lips. His two-day beard growth tickled her skin. "Waiting for you to wake up has been killing me."

Kim shifted to find a more comfortable position, and winced at the burn searing her side.

Ethan stroked the hair from her face. "I'm so sorry I didn't stop Derk before—" He choked on the words.

"As I recall, you told me to take cover," she said, hoping to tease away his remorse. "And I refused to listen."

"You are a stubborn woman. But it's one of the things I love most about you."

Her heart jumped from her chest. *Love? Did he just say love?* She searched his eyes for confirmation.

A hint of insecurity darkened his gaze as he nodded yes.

Grinning stupidly, she reached for his cheek, but immediately winced in pain.

Ethan's expression turned fierce. "What were you thinking, stepping in front of that gun?"

She dug her fingers into his shirt and tugged him closer, this time mindful not to jar her injured side. "I was thinking that I couldn't bear to lose you."

He stilled, a stunned expression on his face.

"Every time Derk threatened to kill me, all I could think of was you." She took a deep breath. "And that I'd never be able to tell you how much you mean to me."

"Oh, sweetheart, I was so afraid I wouldn't find you in time."

She cupped his face in her hands. "But you did. You saved me."

He gently folded her in his arms, his heart thundering against her ear. "You've got it wrong. You saved me. The first day at the manor, when I found you lying in the ditch, something inside me sparked to life. You made me want to be so much more than just a cop. Your absolute acceptance made me believe God has forgiven me. I'm done living in regret. Who am I to tell God that I don't deserve the good things He brings into my life?" He pressed his lips to her hair and tightened his hold.

She pressed her hand to his chest, lifting her gaze to his, and shivered at the love shining there. "Trust me, you deserve them all."

"You are so precious to me. Please know that I would never do anything to hurt you."

"I know, Ethan. Deep down, I've always known, even when I accused you of using me to help your investigation."

He touched his lips to hers and whispered, "I love you." Then he kissed her slowly, deeply, as if trying to put all his love for her into that one kiss. She kissed him back with all the love brimming in her heart.

EPILOGUE

At the sight of cars overflowing the church parking lot, tears sprang to Kim's eyes. But she didn't want to cry today. Joy had organized this memorial to commemorate Dad's service to the community. Today was about celebrating his life, not grieving his death.

Ethan reached across the car's seat and squeezed her hand. "Are you okay?"

"I hadn't expected this many people."

"Blake contacted all the former residents he could find."

"Blake?"

"Yup. After he came out of the coma and told the police what he knew about Derk, I told him that you knew he was the one that ran you off the road, but you refused to press charges. Your concern for his future made quite an impression on him."

Her heart twisted. Thanks to her, Blake had been shot. If she'd reported him in the first place as Ethan had urged, she could've spared him permanent brain damage. "I guess it's just as well the government won't renew Hope Manor's contract. I'm probably too soft-hearted for this work."

"You're wrong. God's given you a special gift for working with those kids."

She lifted her gaze to the cloudless blue sky. If that was true, why hadn't God helped her save the manor?

Mom tapped the car window, Darryl at her side, looking

much happier now that he'd come clean, even with his sentencing pending. "Are you two coming?"

They walked into the auditorium together and took the place reserved for them in the front row. Aaron, Tony and a dozen more Hope Manor employees filled the row behind them. Kim's resolve to not cry dissolved into a puddle as former residents went to the podium and shared the impact Dad had had on each of their lives. At some point, TV cameras arrived. A number of uniformed officers were among the crowd. The police chief even rose to speak. But the biggest surprise of all came when a government official made his way to the podium.

"As you know, there has been much debate of late about the future of Hope Manor. However, a few days ago the organizer of this service informed me that since Mr. Corbett's death, memorial donations in support of Hope Manor have poured in. And I'm here today to tell you that in light of the overwhelming community support, I have secured a renewed ten-year contract for Hope Manor's rehabilitation services to the prison board."

A cheer went up from the crowd.

Darryl reached across the pew and gave Kim a hug. "You did it, sis."

Kim's heart felt ready to burst. She turned to Ethan, but Aaron leaned forward between them.

"Congratulations, Kim. I'm happy you got what you wanted."

"This is good news for you, too. Your job is secure."

Aaron's gaze slid to Ethan before answering. "You haven't heard? I resigned. Got a better offer. PR director of a Fortune 500 company out of Toronto."

"Toronto? You're leaving us?"

For an instant, he seemed pleased by her dismay, but then he shrugged it off. "It was an offer I couldn't refuse." He lifted her hand from the back of the pew and pressed his lips to her fingers. "I'm only sorry it means leaving you. It's been a pleasure working with you."

"Don't you have a train to catch, Sheppard?" Ethan grunted.

Aaron's chin jutted up, but he made his way to the end of the pew.

Kim stared after him in confusion. "What was that about?"

"After I showed him a few photos I took at the beach, he resigned from his position."

She gasped. "You didn't!"

"I didn't think he had the integrity needed for the job. He agreed."

"But what will we do now?" Kim glanced at the faces of her fellow workers making their way to the auditorium for refreshments. As much as she admired each one, she couldn't imagine any of them capable of filling Dad's shoes.

Ethan nudged her attention back to him. "Hope Manor's board of directors asked me to take over your father's job."

"Oh, Ethan," she squealed. "You'll be perfect."

He caught her hands. "I haven't said yes."

"But you will."

His thumb skittered across the back of her hand, and she realized he was trembling. He glanced at the people milling about them. "This isn't where I wanted to have this conversation."

Confused by his sudden frown, her lips trembled into an awkward smile. "Ethan, you're scaring me."

"Kim, I love you. You know that."

At his hesitation, she squared her jaw, bracing for the *but*.

"But I don't think I could bear seeing you every day if…" He scraped his fingers through his hair. "What I'm trying to say is I want to spend the rest of my life with you."

The tender emotion in his voice took her breath away.

He cupped her face. "Not just as a coworker, but as your husband." He whisked her damp cheek with his thumb. "Please tell me those are happy tears."

"Yes! Oh, yes."

He brushed his lips across hers, his eyes beaming a longing to let them linger. Then he folded her into his arms, and as she laid her head against his chest, she thought she heard him whisper, "Thank You, Lord."

* * * * *

Dear Reader,

Readers often ask me where I get my story ideas. The idea for this story came from listening to our pastor's daughter share, at an evening get-together, stories from her time working as a youth-care worker at a detention facility. What struck me the most from her story was her admission that she often learned more from the kids than the other way around. Her enthusiasm for her work and her excitement about the positive impact she could have on residents' lives was the inspiration for my heroine's character and occupation. I hasten to add that while Beth graciously answered all my questions about her work, my heroine is entirely fictional, as is the detention center where she works and the cast of characters who populate her world.

I admire those who can engage others in conversation so naturally, exuding genuine interest and empathy. And I wanted my hero to be smitten by my heroine's empathy and challenged to reconsider his own misperceptions of the residents and himself.

I'd love to hear from you. Join the conversation about the characters in this book and about life in general at www.sandraorchard.blogspot.com. You can also reach me via email at SandraOrchard@ymail.com or by snail mail c/o Harlequin Love Inspired Suspense, 233 Broadway, Suite 1001, New York, NY 10279. To learn about upcoming books, please visit me online at www.sandraorchard.com or www.Facebook.com/SandraOrchard.

Wishing you abundant blessings,
Sandra Orchard

Questions for Discussion

1. Ethan comes to see that while God and those Ethan has hurt offer their forgiveness, he will only be truly freed from the guilt that haunts him if he forgives himself. Are you gripped by guilt over something you've done? What might you do to be freed from that guilt?

2. Because of Kim's unhappy experience with the guy she thought wanted to marry her, she's wary of becoming too attached to another. The moment a guy starts getting serious, she cuts him loose. How have you let past experiences control how you respond to others? How might we overcome such fears?

3. Kim's mom talks about how she didn't want her husband to go to the police when she was pregnant with Kim because she was afraid he'd be arrested and she'd be left alone. Do you regret a past choice you've made? Why or why not?

4. Ethan remarks that the residents always claim incidents are never their fault. When you make a mistake in your life do you tend to blame someone else or do you take responsibility for your actions?

5. Curt, the boy who defended his mom against his father's abuse, hides his pain and insecurity behind a tough, "I'm okay" exterior. Do you know someone like that? How might you reach out to show them you care about what's troubling them?

6. Kim wants to believe the best of everyone. How does that make her good at her job? How might it endanger her?

How might others benefit if you were quicker to believe the best of someone rather than the worst?

7. Kim tells Ethan that Joy brings a heart full of hope and joy to those she counsels whereas Ethan brings a heart full of sadness and regret. What's in your heart? Are you happy with its condition? If not, what can you do to become more joy-filled?

8. Darryl let his mother talk him into doing something he knew was wrong, but that he felt would be okay since they had a noble reason. Is there ever justification for doing something contrary to the law—God's or your country's? Why or why not?

9. Unable to face her father's approaching death, Kim throws her energy into trying to preserve the work to which he's devoted his life. Her brother tells her she's only trying to hold on to their Dad and that it won't work. Is there something in your life that you don't want to face? Why? What's the worst that would happen if you did? Do you believe God is big enough to carry you through the worst?

10. Kim ministers to youths from various troubled backgrounds. Have you ever had the opportunity to reach out to a troubled teen? How did it affect your life and the teen's?

INSPIRATIONAL

SUSPENSE

COMING NEXT MONTH
AVAILABLE APRIL 10, 2012

UNDERCOVER BODYGUARD
Heroes for Hire
Shirlee McCoy
With a stalker after her, Shelby Simons
needs a bodyguard—but does it have to
be this gorgeous former SEAL?

THE WIDOW'S PROTECTOR
Fitzgerald Bay
Stephanie Newton

RACE AGAINST TIME
Christy Barritt

AT ANY COST
Lauren Nichols

REQUEST YOUR FREE BOOKS!

2 FREE RIVETING INSPIRATIONAL NOVELS
PLUS 2 FREE MYSTERY GIFTS

Love Inspired®
SUSPENSE

YES! Please send me 2 FREE Love Inspired® Suspense novels and my 2 FREE mystery gifts (gifts are worth about $10). After receiving them, if I don't wish to receive any more books, I can return the shipping statement marked "cancel". If I don't cancel, I will receive 4 brand-new novels every month and be billed just $4.49 per book in the U.S. or $4.99 per book in Canada. That's a saving of at least 22% off the cover price. It's quite a bargain! Shipping and handling is just 50¢ per book in the U.S. and 75¢ per book in Canada.* I understand that accepting the 2 free books and gifts places me under no obligation to buy anything. I can always return a shipment and cancel at any time. Even if I never buy another book, the two free books and gifts are mine to keep forever.

123/323 IDN FEHR

Name	(PLEASE PRINT)

Address	Apt. #

City	State/Prov.	Zip/Postal Code

Signature (if under 18, a parent or guardian must sign)

Mail to the **Reader Service:**
IN U.S.A.: P.O. Box 1867, Buffalo, NY 14240-1867
IN CANADA: P.O. Box 609, Fort Erie, Ontario L2A 5X3

Not valid for current subscribers to Love Inspired Suspense books.

**Are you a subscriber to Love Inspired Suspense
and want to receive the larger-print edition?
Call 1-800-873-8635 or visit www.ReaderService.com.**

* Terms and prices subject to change without notice. Prices do not include applicable taxes. Sales tax applicable in N.Y. Canadian residents will be charged applicable taxes. Offer not valid in Quebec. This offer is limited to one order per household. All orders subject to credit approval. Credit or debit balances in a customer's account(s) may be offset by any other outstanding balance owed by or to the customer. Please allow 4 to 6 weeks for delivery. Offer available while quantities last.

Your Privacy—The Reader Service is committed to protecting your privacy. Our Privacy Policy is available online at www.ReaderService.com or upon request from the Reader Service.

We make a portion of our mailing list available to reputable third parties that offer products we believe may interest you. If you prefer that we not exchange your name with third parties, or if you wish to clarify or modify your communication preferences, please visit us at www.ReaderService.com/consumerschoice or write to us at Reader Service Preference Service, P.O. Box 9062, Buffalo, NY 14269. Include your complete name and address.

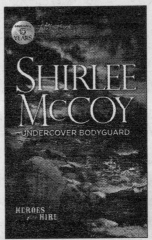

For a sneak peek of Shirlee McCoy's heart-stopping inspirational romantic suspense
UNDERCOVER BODYGUARD, read on!

"It's okay," Ryder said, pulling Shelby into his arms.

But it wasn't okay, and they both knew it.

A woman was dead, and there was nothing either of them could do to change it.

"How can it be when Maureen is dead?" Shelby asked, looking up into his face as if he might have some way to fix things. He didn't, and he'd stopped believing in his own power and invincibility long ago.

"It will be. Eventually. Come on. You need to get the bump on your head looked at."

"I don't have time for that. I have to get back to the bakery. It's Friday. The busiest day of the week." Her teeth chattered on the last word, her body trembling. He draped his coat around her shoulders.

"Better?" he asked, and she nodded.

"I can't seem to stop shaking. I mean, one minute, I'm preparing to deliver pastries to my friend and the next she's gone. I just can't believe...." Her voice trailed off, her eyes widening as she caught sight of his gun holster.

"You've got a gun."

"Yes."

"Are you a police officer?"

"Security contractor."

"You're a bodyguard?"

"I'm a security contractor. I secure people and things."

"A bodyguard," she repeated, and he didn't argue.

Two fire trucks and an ambulance lined the curb in front of the house, and firefighters had already hooked a hose to the hydrant. Water streamed over the flames but did little to douse the fire.

Suddenly, an EMT ran toward them. "Is she okay?"

"She was knocked unconscious by the force of the explosion. She has a bad gash on her head."

"Let me take a look." The EMT edged him out of the way, and Ryder knew it was time to go talk to the fire marshal and the police officers who'd just arrived, and let the EMT take Shelby to the hospital.

But she grabbed his hand before he moved away, her grip surprisingly strong. "Are you leaving?"

"Do you want me to, Shelby Ann?" he asked.

"You can leave."

"I know that I can, but do you *want* me to?"

"I…haven't decided, yet."

Pick up UNDERCOVER BODYGUARD for the rest of Shelby and Ryder's exciting, suspenseful love story, available in April 2012, only from Love Inspired® Books Love Inspired® Suspense.